THE
RESURRECTIONIST

THE
RESURRECTIONIST

THE LOST WORK
OF
DR. SPENCER BLACK

BY E. B. HUDSPETH

QUIRK BOOKS

PHILADELPHIA

Copyright © 2013 by Eric Hudspeth
All rights reserved. No part of this book may be reproduced
in any form without written permission from the publisher.
Library of Congress Cataloging in Publication Number: 2012934523
ISBN: 978-1-59474-616-1

Printed in China
Typeset in Bodoni and Sabon

Designed by Doogie Horner
Production management by John J. McGurk

Quirk Books
215 Church Street
Philadelphia, PA 19106
quirkbooks.com

10 9 8 7 6 5 4

resurrectionist *n* (14c) **1** an exhumer and
stealer of corpses; a resurrection man
2 one who revives or brings to light again
[f. RESURRECTION sb. + -IST. Hence F.
resurrectionniste.]

A Note from the Publisher

THIS BOOK WOULD NOT exist without the tireless efforts and generous financial support of Philadelphia's Museum of Medical Antiquities.

Over the past fifteen years, their curators have toured private collections throughout the United States and Europe in search of the lost journals, letters, and illustrations of Dr. Spencer Black, one of the most remarkable physicians and scientific mavericks Western civilization has ever known.

As most physicians and students of medicine undoubtedly already know, Dr. Black achieved fame and notoriety in the late nineteenth century for his pioneering work in treating genetic abnormalities. No one disputes that Dr. Black was a genuine prodigy; before he had even reached the age of twenty-one, his work was known by surgeons around the world. And yet this professional acclaim was short-lived. Much of Dr. Black's later work remains shrouded in controversy, rumors, and whispers of blasphemous abominations. Thanks to the materials collected herein, we now know that Dr. Black's personal and professional exploits were far more scandalous than anything found in the gothic novels that were popular during his lifetime.

Many of the letters and illustrations in this book were donated from the estate of Dr. Black's brother, Bernard. These materials have been unseen since the International Convention of Modern Science in 1938 (where their display was fleeting, because of public disapproval). Other letters, journals, and drawings have come to us directly from anonymous donors, and these are published here for the first time. They offer startling new insights into the doctor's personal life and professional achievements.

This publication begins with the most complete biography to date of the Western world's most controversial surgeon. It is followed by a near-complete reproduction of Dr. Black's magnum opus, *The Codex Extinct Animalia*.

Together, these two extraordinary documents are the definitive study of Dr. Spencer Black. They are *The Resurrectionist*.

THE LIFE

OF

DR. SPENCER

BLACK

1851–1868

CHILDHOOD

*In my childish imagination, God's wrathful arm was
ever-ready and ever-present.*
—Spencer Black

Dr. Spencer Black and his older brother, Bernard, were born in Boston, Massachusetts, in 1851 and 1848, respectively. They were the sons of the renowned surgeon Gregory Black. Their mother, Meredith Black, died while delivering Spencer; her passing caused a great unrest in both boys throughout their childhood.

Gregory Black was a respected professor of anatomy at the Medical Arts College of Boston. He conducted dissections for students at a time when cadavers were scarce and anatomists depended on grave-robbing resurrectionists to further their research. He had some of his favorite cadavers preserved, dressed, and propped up in a macabre anthropomorphic display in his office. As one of the city's leading professors, with an increasing number of students every year, his demand for bodies surpassed the legal supply. He was one of the primary purchasers of stolen cadavers in the area, and he dug up many additional bodies himself, with the assistance of his two young sons. Spencer Black writes at length about these experiences in his journals.

*I was no older than eleven when the ordeal began. The night
I remember above all, I was hurried out of bed after my brother,
Bernard: my elder by three years. He was always stirred awake
first so he could help prepare the horse and tie up the cart.*

Hours before dawn, in the cool of the night, we walked

away from our home and went down to the river where we could cross a bridge; beyond which the road was dark and obscured, an excellent place to enter and leave the cemetery unnoticed.

We were all quiet, for calling attention to ourselves would have done us no service. It was damp and wet that night: it had rained earlier and I could smell water still fresh in the air. We slowly moved along the bridge. I remember the wheels of the cart, straining and creaking, threatening to arouse the nearby residents and their curiosities with just one sudden noise. Steam rose off our aged horse. The mist of her breath was comforting; she was an innocent creature—our accomplice. The narrow stream below, too dark to see, trickled quietly. Any sound that we made with our dreary march was muted as soon as we crossed the bridge and went over the moss-covered earth framing the cemetery. Once inside the perimeter my father was at ease, his humor improved, and with a calm gaiety he led us to a newly established residence for some deceased soul. They called us resurrectionists, grave robbers.

When I was a child I hadn't the conviction against the belief in God that I have now. My father was not a religious man, however my grandparents were, and they gave me a rigorous theological education. I was very much afraid of what we did those nights; of all the terrible sins a man might commit, stealing the dead seemed among the worst. In my childish imagination, God's wrathful arm was ever-ready and ever-present. And yet I feared my father even more than I feared my God.

My father reminded us there was no cause for trepidation or fear. He would repeat these things as we dug through the night, as the smell of the body's decay rose around us. Soon we reached the soft, damp, wood coffin of Jasper Earl Werthy. The wood cracked, releasing more of death's repugnant odor. I put my spade down, grateful that my father was wrenching the wood and freeing the body himself, sparing us this task. Jasper's face was a sunken gray mask; his skin was like a rotten orange. This is how I came to understand my father's profession.

Soon afterward, Dr. Black penned another journal entry with a short poem titled "A Dreadful Sight." The poem appears to be inspired by his experiences robbing graves.

It is the only known work of poetry found among Dr. Black's papers and reflects a creative impulse that manifested itself in his numerous illustrations.

A Dreadful Sight

I went to rest one merry night,
On the morrow was a dreadful sight.
My dear loved one has passed away.
So to the coffin she must stay.
In the earth where 'tis quiet and calm
to rest in peace till the Lord has come.
I go to visit, weep and mourn.
Lo' my loved one's body has gone.
Not to heaven where she belongs
but from the grave to the doctor's room.

In the winter of 1868, Spencer Black's father, Gregory, died from smallpox, a disease that some say he would have been brilliant enough to cure had he been given forewarning. Soon after the funeral, Spencer announced his decision to become a medical doctor. It's clear throughout Black's writings that he thought of death as an abstract concept; he often calls death "the phenomenon of the living" and even regarded the passing of his own father as more of a curiosity than a tragedy.

> *As he lay in the ground, and the dirt and the sod were laid*
> *over him, all was quiet. I waited for a long space of time. I waited*
> *to hear something: a command or suggestion, a provocation that*
> *might confirm that his death took something away from me, but I*
> *received no such thing.*

Bernard Black kept a separate journal of his life and work in the natural sciences until his disappearance in 1908. His wife, Emma, published some of his writings in her book entitled *A Journey with an American Naturalist*. This entry was written in the same week as the patriarch's death:

> *At that moment, when I had a great and heavy pain that was*
> *suffered upon me by our father's death, I could see Spencer at that*

very identical moment looked exalted. He leapt into my father's grave with all his heart, chasing after death to seek out its hiding place.

After the passing of their father, Spencer and Bernard moved to Philadelphia in the fall of 1869 and were placed in the care of their uncle Zacariah and aunt Isadore. The funerary costs were quite extensive; Gregory had set some money aside for his burial, but it was not enough. Zacariah and Isadore paid the balance out of their savings, and it was likely a significant sum. Then, as now, a proper burial came at a high price.

1869

THE ACADEMY OF MEDICINE

*The truth is a commodity that is rarely distributed
in these empirical times. What evidence can be given
that the sun is bright on both of its sides? I cannot
prove this, so is it thusly untrue?*
*—Sir Vincent Holmes, biologist, founder of the
Academy of Medicine*

Prior to moving to Philadelphia, Bernard had already completed three years of schooling at the Medical Arts College of Boston, whereas Spencer had completed just one. Both young men enrolled in Philadelphia's Academy of Medicine to continue their studies. It was during this year that Spencer began keeping his journal.

September 1869

What a miracle it is to be human! I endeavor to write this account of my life, the chronicling of my study and experience with the Academy of Medicine here in Philadelphia—not my place of birth. It was not by my choosing that I would pursue a career in medicine—this is a matter of fate, God, destiny, or some other weapon of man.

I was born of good and well-educated parents, both of whom are now gone. My mother died delivering birth to me while my father attended. He held my life in one hand and her death in the other. He did not often speak of her.

It was in the winter of my sixteenth year when my father succumbed to smallpox: a disease that took his life. I am certain that I mourned my father's death; however, I did not weep.

As he lay in his coffin, I thought he may likely rise again. He may come out of the hole, bundled in rags by unknown men with faces obscured by darkness and soot or ash. He would then be dragged down the path and loaded into a cart. A few seconds would pass, then the reigns would snap and the horse would carry him away. My father was a well-known and respected doctor and anatomist. He certainly paid for many corpses for his research; now he too may serve science yet again.

When one dies they neither ascend to the heavens nor descend to hell, they instead become cured—freed from an illness and healed from the suffering of mortality. Our consciousness, our awareness, is a symptom of our body and it is secondary to the mystery of our physical chemistry. It is in this sincere application to biology where I promise to excel as a scientist of medicine. The entire body is the soul, and my knife cuts deep into the flesh; I vow to be always reverent with the edge of my scalpel.

Spencer Black excelled at the Academy of Medicine. It was evident to both his peers and his teachers that he would soon be a fledgling practitioner in the medical arts. Noted for being extremely serious and clever for his age, Spencer made a name for himself as one of the most promising prodigies in the country. Bernard's interests were quite different: he had decided to focus his work on the natural sciences, fossils, and history.

One of Spencer's most influential professors was Joseph Warren Denkel, a Scottish immigrant who first studied at the Medical Arts College of Boston, where he met Spencer's father as a fellow student. He later worked as a field surgeon during the Civil War, performing hundreds of amputations; many of these resulted in death by infection. At Philadelphia's Academy of Medicine, Denkel was perceived as a charismatic physician, often jocular with staff and patients, prone to gambling and other raucous behavior in the evenings. He and Spencer Black became good friends.

During this time in American medicine great and dramatic changes were occurring rapidly throughout not only this country but the world as well. Physicians were beginning to understand bacteria and its role in infection. Sanitation practices were improving. The practice of washing hands or dipping them in carbolic acid was increasingly common, replacing older notions that dried blood on surgeons' hands acted as a sanitary barrier or that sanitation had no correlation to infection during surgery. The introduction of anesthesia revolutionized surgery; it allowed the surgeon more time to perform the work without worrying about the patient's pain. Black welcomed these advancements and was excited about contributing ideas of his own.

During his first year at the academy, in 1869, Black began to research mutations of the body—specifically, physical abnormalities that manifest in dramatic, unique, and even fatal ways. However, studying people maligned with these conditions was not easy. They often died early or were difficult to find because they were secluded from the public. Much of Black's early work was influenced by his experiences at the Grossemier Museum in downtown Philadelphia. In the museum's collection was a famously peculiar skeleton of parapagus dicephalus dibrachius (conjoined twins); the skeleton was named Ella and Emily; the girls had died at birth. He wrote his first paper about their unfortunate condition. The result was highly praised but not well distributed; much of Black's work was considered less worthy of discussion than the research of infectious diseases, more efficient surgical practice, or improved anesthesia. Many thought the young doctor was wasting his time on birth defects. Black wrote about some of his frustrations during that time:

> *I am engrossed in anatomical research now. Denkel is assisting my efforts despite what other professors have called, "unnecessary and fruitless interests in mutations of the body." He is either ignorant of their counsel or genuinely interested in my research—I tend to think it's the latter.*
>
> *The miracle of life is granted, and how that miracle can be defective is a nuance that I am most interested in understanding. Denkel and I are preparing another article for publication this spring. I trust it should prove quite insightful.*

Spencer Black began taking illustration seriously during his first year at the academy. It was not uncommon for doctors to sketch their notes and findings, but Black was excessively good at the practice, and he found work in the evenings drawing the work of other researchers. One of these was the renowned botanist and traveler Jean DeLain.

DeLain's collection was kept at the Broadshire University Atrium, where Black would often go to study. He would continue to work for DeLain off and on for many years, illustrating hundreds of specimens for him.

English Yew
Taxus baccata

Myrrh
Commiphora myrrh

Lily of the Valley
Convallaria majalis

Three of the plants that Spencer Black illustrated for the botanist Jean DeLain; all are well known for their distinct properties.

The English Yew bears a seed that is extremely poisonous. The tree can live for more than two thousand years; some are believed to be as old as nine thousand years. In certain spiritual circles, the yew is celebrated for its transcendence of death. Its resilience has inspired many cultures to revere it as a symbol of rebirth and everlasting life.

Myrrh is the tree from which the reddish-brown gum resin is derived; it is famous among Christians for being one of the three gifts bestowed on the infant Jesus. Myrrh is a well-known incense and is still used for its aromatic and medicinal qualities.

Lily of the Valley, extremely poisonous, has many stories and legends ascribed to it. Also known as Our Lady's Tears, the plant is believed to have sprung from the tears of Mary while she wept at the crucifixion of her son Jesus Christ. It is believed that the plant can grant the power to envision a better world. It also symbolizes the return of happiness, or the return of Jesus Christ.

Figure 1. *Actias luna-male*   Luna Moth
Figure 2. *Papilio machaon*   Swallowtail Butterfly
Figure 3. *Parnassius apollo*   Apollo (Mountain Apollo) Butterfly
Figure 4. *Pomponia imperatoria*   Empress Cicada

I am making notable improvements in my illustrations. What a reprieve from words and lectures. I can study, think, and relax more while taking care to lavish in the solitude of drawing.

Spencer Black also wrote about many of the insects and plants that he studied. He was particularly interested in insects that underwent a metamorphosis. The process of transformation fascinated the young scientist, and he often sketched the cicada and made regular mention of it in his journals and letters.

November 22, 1869

In the summer, when the cicadas emerge from the ground, they transform into a winged insect, sing their song, mate, lay eggs, and soon die. The pupae hatch from their eggs in a tree then fall to the ground and burrow deep into the earth, where they live for more than a decade.

Such evanescence; to emerge from the ground after such a long time and then transform, gaining wings. They are born once again from the womb of their own body, which is abandoned as an empty shell, and then they leave the world. This type of metamorphosis (though not as dramatic as that of the butterfly or moth, in a superficial context) is, in my esteem, one of the more significant. After such a long time in darkness, we can live for only a short while.

* * *

December 1, 1869

I have become interested in a different assignment given to me by Professor Jean DeLain. He needs several illustrations of small and curious insects illustrated for a book he is compiling; the insects gathered are all dead, carefully packed and pinned. They have arrived from many locations of the world: Guinea, the Malaysian islands, Africa and Asia. It is exciting to study the smallest differences in their particular designs. There is little separation between man and insect, save the marvels solely unique to their respective functions in nature.

Cicadidæ

Fig 1

Fig 2.

Fig 3

Spencer Black

Figure 1. The pupa stage, freshly emerged from the ground.

Figure 2. The insect emerges from its shell, reborn. It waits to gain its strength.

Figure 3. Now fully developed, the cicada can fly away, sing its song, mate, and the cycle can repeat.

1870

WARD C

*The sustainable body of scientific evidence is derived
from the contractions made by the objective observer,
not the parroting of the learned scholar.*
—Dr. Spencer Black

By the end of his second year at the academy, Spencer was devoting all his time to the mysteries of the human body. He attended as many dissections as possible, whether they were hosted by the academy or by neighboring institutions. It's highly likely that he also performed dissections of his own; some believe that Spencer employed the lessons learned from his childhood to locate and dig up fresh cadavers for research. He never wrote about those experiences, however.

By this time, Bernard had finished his studies and traveled to New York to begin a successful career with the New York Society of Science, but his accomplishments would soon be dwarfed by those of his brother. Even by the age of nineteen, Spencer Black had cemented his reputation as one of the country's brightest young scientists. His motivation, drive, and passion for research are all evident in his journal entries of the year 1870.

February 1870
I am working now, ceaselessly, with no apparent results. I have come to believe there is something greater to learn about anatomy, something more meaningful than a simple physical mutation or flaw in human growth or development. Thus far, in my embryonic research, I cannot discover the source or even

the impetus for such mutations. They aren't sensible; something must be explained or understood prior to their acceptance. We as scientists, physicians, sophists, do not allow such nonsense as god and monsters to infect our logic.

A man walks, he talks, he attacks and he parries. He does all of these wondrous things; and yet some persist in being born unable to do any of them.

I cannot assume that I am going to discover any cause as to why children can be born without arms or why twins are born fused together—why extra fingers and toes can grow, or none can grow at all. Why does the human form exist so? Why not another arrangement? As soon as I can understand this, I will move forward.

I must know why five fingers are intended before I can discover the cause of six.

The questions regarding nature's ability to malfunction disturb me greatly. I never believed in the delineation of God or nature, only that certain laws maintain—one of which is function. I've wrestled with the fallibility of this perfect organism—our body. How can the body, being designed and charged to a specific task, mutate and abandon its function without the fulfillment of another one? These are fundamental principles that cannot be merely glanced at and then disregarded while using barbaric words like "deformed" or "diseased." Simply stating that an object is in disrepair does not allow that object the benefit of a new identity. I now set out to examine the very seed that is the cause of my vexing: Why can the body mutate?

In the spring of 1870, Black began a special surgical program at the Academy of Medicine that was dedicated to the research and improvement of operable birth defects: it was the first of its kind. The intention was to learn how to help those who were afflicted with various deformities, and perhaps to prevent the deformities in future births. Since Joseph Warren Denkel was already mentoring Black, the elder scientist was tasked with overseeing the operation. Also participating was Dr. Joab A. Holace, an American physician renowned for his work on embryonic research and conjoined twins. Black was immediately impressed with Dr. Holace, as is clear from his journal entry dated May 1870:

I have attended lectures of his before and was impressed with his oratory prowess—remarks he simply uttered without consideration resonated as profound revelations. His thoughts seemed preformed, as though he had carefully composed them the night prior but he then gave them out freely, like a wealthy man tossing unwanted change to paupers. There is much to gain from him.

The academy granted the team the use of a separate operating room on the third floor, where there was plenty of light, privacy, and space. This special laboratory would later be known only as Ward C. Privileged with the newest technology—microscopes, chemicals, and tools—Ward C became famous for being one of the most advanced scientific research spaces in the world. It was certainly unique in its specialty.

The team consisted of Denkel (Ward C's administrator), two surgeons (Drs. Black and Holace), and two specialists in human mutations. Their first operation was performed on June 3, 1870. The patient was a young man whose fingers were fused together, a condition known as ectrodactyly, or lobster's claw, because of the hands' appearance. This operation was relatively simple and resulted in success. Later that same summer, the team operated on a young girl born with polydactyly, a condition wherein digits or limbs are duplicated. The young girl had an additional right arm fused directly above her natural right arm, spanning its length from shoulder to fingertips. She appeared to have one large right forearm but eight right fingers and two right thumbs. In a matter of hours the surgeons were able to remove the parasitic arm; the patient healed well. The success of the surgery was published in medical journals throughout the United States and was read via articles in the international press; Dr. Spencer Black was gaining popularity, and his work was considered remarkable.

In the fall of 1870, Black published his controversial paper "The Perfect Human." It states that man is merely the sum of his evolutionary parts. Black claimed that humankind has been "assembled" over time, with occasional pieces added and—more importantly—occasional pieces removed. Unlike the traditionally accepted theories of evolution and natural selection, Black's view stressed that mutations are not accidents; instead, they are the body attempting to grow what it once had thousands of years ago. According to Black, this was the only solution to the dilemmas of teratology (the scientific study of congenital abnormalities and abnormal formations). He argued: "From where else can the knowledge arrive? The body cannot grow something without knowing how."

Among the paper's most controversial claims was the idea that many so-called mythological creatures were in fact real species that once walked the earth. Black further argued that remnants of these creatures sometimes manifested themselves in latent traits, that is, genetic mutations. Dr. Holace, Black's fellow surgeon, strongly disagreed with this claim; it was the beginning of what would become a bitter rivalry.

Despite the negative attention, Black went on to publish two additional papers. One discussed the physical memories of blood, bile, and plasma; the other was a research piece on the mutations of children and how their bodies cope with the changes of growth into adulthood. Both papers included illustrations.

In just a few months' time, news of the extraordinary work being performed in Ward C had spread throughout the global medical community. Soon, the doctors were receiving letters of accommodation and invitations to lecture from all parts of the world. The ward's success in surgery and research had propelled Black into the public arena: he was integral to the reasons for its success.

1871–1877

MARRIAGE AND TRANSFORMATION

Doctors are not gods; but we do their work.
—Dr. Spencer Black

Spencer Black completed his schooling with the highest of honors. Nearing international fame at the remarkably young age of twenty, the precocious doctor was considered an extremely attractive prospect among Philadelphia's most elite families.

Black met Elise Chardelle while she was visiting the academy undertaking research for an anthropological thesis on evolution and natural selection. Little is known about her, but Black's notes suggest that she was attractive, had been well educated, and came from a prosperous family in Chicago. They fell in love almost immediately, and after just three months of courtship the couple married in June 1871.

Unprepared and without having intended to, I proposed marriage.
I do not know how to say what I feel, but it is wonderful.

Through his work in Ward C, Black was earning a substantial salary, and he purchased a rather large home near the academy. In the spring of 1872, Elise gave birth to their first child, Alphonse. He was born healthy and would grow to continue his father's legacy.

Portrait of Elise Chardelle, 1871. Written on the back of the drawing is the following note: *Dearest Elise, As the sun sets now I write this, filled with love and hope for you and a life we will share. I will forever abide, in my heart and by your side, to the love I have for you. Forever yours, Spencer*

Portrait of Alphonse Edward Black. This is the only known image of Alphonse. The handwritten caption reads: *My son Alphonse sleeping. S. Black.* **1872.**

On March 1, 1872, nine months less four days from the date of our marriage, my son, Alphonse, was born in the season of the cicadas.

The medical community and the country as a whole were excited and hopeful for the potential demonstrated by the work being performed in Ward C. The school grounds were overfilled with students, and the academy had to change its curriculum and admittance policies to adapt to its quickly rising prestige. By 1873, applications to the school numbered in the tens of thousands.

Unfortunately, Ward C's successful run was interrupted by the arrival of a nine-year-old patient named Meredith Anne Heath. The girl was born with a parasitic twin; she had an additional two legs and an arm extending from her abdomen. She had traveled with her family from Colorado to Ward C to receive an operation. Only a few minutes into the surgical procedure, complications arose; after forty-five minutes of extremely painful surgery, Meredith died. Although Dr. Holace claimed culpability for the tragedy, it was deemed unpreventable, uncontrollable, and unforeseeable by the academy's medical council. Black shared in the feelings of guilt.

March 12, 1873

It was not my knife, but lo, were we not all present at the death? I cannot accept that we could not have prevented the very thing we caused. We cut her, and the blood spilled out. It's the very opposite of what I intended: I wish to deal in salvation, not death. Her family, parents, and brothers returned home. A shroud and maybe a coffin with a little stain, if they can afford it, will carry the child. What manner of physician shall I become? How often will I encounter death?

The loss had a strong effect on Black, and his relationship with his colleagues seemed shaken. It was the latest in a long series of disagreements with his onetime mentor, Dr. Joab A. Holace.

I suppose I can understand his strict and linear approach to medical science, but I believe the journal of laws needs to be held lightly so that one may easily read from it when needed, but may also let go and be freed from its weight in an instant.

Black resented the failure, and (for reasons not entirely clear) he blamed Holace and the staff of Ward C for the girl's death. It is possible that Black was wrestling with personal issues; he wrote often of nightmares and nervousness, both of which may have contributed to the failure of his professional relationships.

> *Again, I dreamt last night that a cadaver was brought into the dissection theater. When the cloth was lifted from the body, I saw the sunken face of my father. Then, in their aprons, they began cutting and removing pieces of him; when they finished, everyone left the auditorium. I looked and saw that he was dead but his organs remained alive—his vibrant heart trembling, his kidneys excreting fluid. And then I awoke.*

In the fall of 1874, Black suffered the anguish of death once again—only this time, it arrived close to home. His wife, Elise, bore another child, Elizabeth, who tragically succumbed only a few days later to organ failure. By all accounts, Black was devastated by the loss.

Yet he continued his work in Ward C. Over the next four years, from 1874 through 1878, Black consistently proved himself an asset to his colleagues and made tremendous advancements in grafting, vivisection, and correctional surgery. These achievements raised the reputation of the academy to unparalleled heights.

> *Never before has a medical arts center delivered on so many of their optimistic promises as has the Academy of Medicine in Philadelphia. The young student is certain to gain a qualified and most beneficial education while studying within those walls.*
> —Alfred J. J. Strong, M.D., New York

Elise gave birth to another child, Victor, in the winter of 1876, but the boy's arrival scarcely merits a mention in Black's journals. The doctor, now twenty-five years old, was changing. Once energetic, he had become morose and cynical; many claimed that his eccentric and erratic behavior made him an increasingly difficult personality. He also suffered from a volatile temper and a quick impatience with differing opinions. The burgeoning strength in his convictions that had made him famous only a few years earlier was now working against him; his reputation at the academy and even his prosperity were in jeopardy. Still, his devotion to his research never flagged. He was so busy that he began to neglect his friends, family, and professional obligations to the academy.

> *The frost of autumn becomes the storm of winter. I cannot rest my mind in a place of tranquil thought. I am left to contemplate my childhood and drudge through its ugliness. I would be very pleased with a warm spring day and a sun-soaked room to work in, instead of this wet and grayed tapestry of nature's dead season. Perhaps my spirits would be lifted if the faces I see daily were not also gray and dead.*

During 1877, his last year in Ward C, Black worked less and less at the academy while devoting increasing amounts of his attention to private studies. He developed new, polarizing ideas regarding evolution that would ultimately separate him from the rest of the scientific community. At twenty-six years of age, he wrote notes and theories entertaining the notion that through evolution and certain paths of natural selection, humans had lost some of their natural and necessary traits. The lack of these critical elements, he believed, resulted in mutations and deformities.

Furthermore, Black speculated that perhaps the human being is not the best result of evolution; perhaps our ancestors shared traits with some of the ancient animals or, more accurately, ancient mythological animals. Black claimed that scientific evidence proving the existence of ancient mythological animals had been concealed by unnamed parties; taxonomy records were destroyed, constellation records were changed, fairy tales were altered and rewritten, all in an attempt to ignore our true history. Though Black never blamed anyone specifically for this grand conspiracy, it seems he had a certain individual (or individuals) in mind.

All of Ward C's success and recognition appeared inconsequential to Dr. Black; he seemed to believe that the culmination of his work was incomplete. In this journal entry he had already resigned himself to pursue his less-popular theories, even though he had no idea how to do so. It would take an unexpected encounter at a carnival sideshow before he would fully mature into the study of teratology.

> *July 1877*
> *And now, in the dawn of great discoveries, the dreary and rotten can be laid to the wayside. I must plow forward and*

continue my work, research, and growth if I am to contribute anything more than a few meager surgeries.

There is so much more to be done. We at the Ward are only butchers and tailors—we are not yet healers. I wish to find the means to isolate the problem in order to eliminate subtractive surgery entirely. One who bears the weight of medical insight upon his conscience knows too well that life is not a consequence of nature but instead its most precious and coveted secret. Nature governs its creations equally; a man can perish as easily as a plant can be destroyed beneath one's heel.

1878

THE FAWN-CHILD

*Alphonse is growing so wonderfully, like a plant in
the spring. What a miracle, what a machine; I am
increasingly grateful for his healthy deliverance into
the world.*
—Dr. Spencer Black

D r. Spencer Black's career and aspirations changed after he paid a visit to a
local carnival (the exact name of which remains unknown). Featured among
the giants, acrobats, and other "marvels of nature" roaming the sideshows
was an anatomy museum—an exhibit of strange medical artifacts and bizarre biological
specimens.

The anatomy museums, along with cabinets of curiosities, had been popular
scientific novelty collections for hundreds of years; many of these grand accumulations
are still available for public view. It was this show that eclipsed Black's previous work and
inspired him to study what would become one of the most bizarre and unique pursuits of
any scientist, least of all one with his talents.

> *These sideshows, of which I have seen many, are typically decrepit
> affairs leaving one with a great thirst for civility, men, and manners.
> The performers are often subjects of ridicule and humiliation, and
> they usually become patients of mine in the Ward—seeking a better
> life or, at the least, humanity.*

The show was primarily a showcase of well-known abnormalities with a few less-common defects of the human form. The collection included a skeleton of conjoined twins, fused at the skull; the monster-baby (a pig fetus in a jar); and the South Pacific mermaid (a monkey and trout sewn together). All the displays were easily identified by anyone familiar with science and medicine. The exception was the fawn-child, a deceased young boy displaying an orthopedic condition that had caused his knees to bend the wrong way. The bones were misshapen, and excessive hair was present over the entire surface of the skin; there were bone or calcium growths at the top of his skull, which gave the appearance of juvenile horns. The dead child was preserved in a large alcohol-filled glass jar.

Black was convinced that the specimen held a secret to his research. He believed that the mutations were manifestations of the ancient past he had written about—evidence of a genetic code that was not completely eradicated. Some have argued that Black found answers in places where there was no need for questions. Whatever the case, the encounter with the fawn-child fueled his obsession for finding a cure for the deformation that was paramount in his work. He would never again practice conventional medicine.

The promoter of the sideshow sold the specimen to Black for two hundred dollars, a small fortune. Black took the fawn-child home and conducted a secret but thorough dissection in the attic. Not even his family knew of his work until it was completed.

What is interesting is that in his writings and notes, Black expressed that he was not working on a human being who had suffered from deformation. Rather, he believed the fawn-child was exhibiting a vestige of a mythological past. His approach to anatomy and medicine had changed dramatically in a rather short amount of time.

August 14, 1878

My dissection thus far has revealed nothing that would lead me to think this was not a relative to a satyr. I have brought a small common domestic goat (Capra domestica) up to the attic to use for comparison. My tests determine that there is indeed an animal woven into the fawn-child; however, it is not related to this particular type of goat. Discovering the relative will not be easy; the differences in size, color, and horns make it difficult to determine relationships. The fawn-child bears a resemblance to the ibex (Capra ibex), one of the more perfect goats, but its fur is like that of the cashmere goat (Capra thibetensis).

Physiologically, the animal is human, it does not have the four chambered stomach of other ruminants; therefore, I have not found a bezoar stone either. It is human . . . mostly.

I am trying to hold firm to reason and logic while I learn a lifetime of zoological science in a mere month. I am trying not to perform an injustice to the innocent creature on my table. I am fighting fatigue and sickness daily now: the anxiety of this work and knowledge is weighing heavily. My nerves are ruined, but oddly I feel vitalized and nourished at the same time. I cannot think, I cannot eat or sleep, smile or be angry; I feel nothing other than a nauseating compulsion to continue the work on the flayed creature who silently waits in the attic. With its skin peeled back and pinned in place, its organs removed and floating in jars of noxious liquid; it waits beside drawings and notes documenting its total and final destruction.

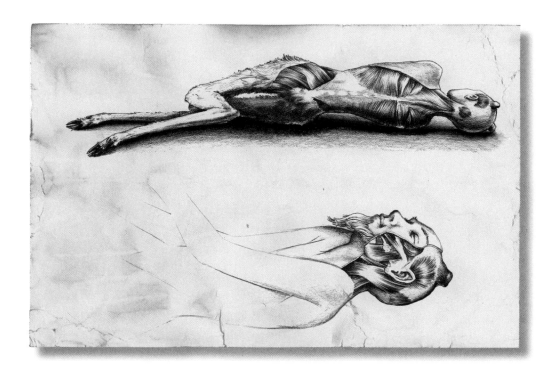

Drawing made by Spencer Black during the early stages of dissecting the fawn-child. Philadelphia, 1878.

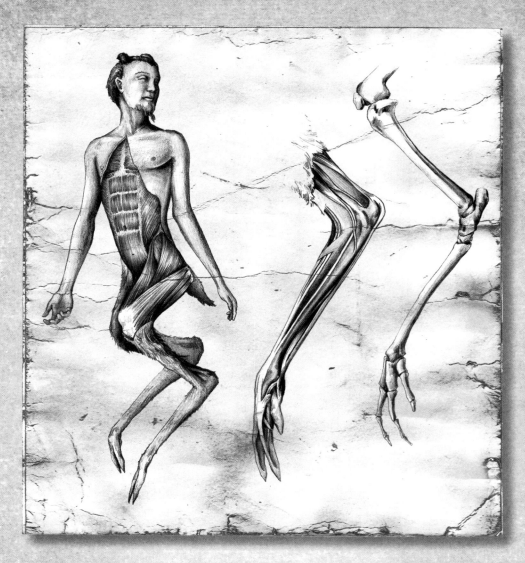

In these details, the genetic deformation is illustrated more clearly, and it's easy to see why this condition might generate such interest in the nineteenth century, or even today. In his notes on the dissection, Dr. Black writes: *I positioned the body transverse and squarely on its back. I then prepared the side table and logbook for notes to record the first session of the dissection. I will continue carefully; I will make notes of everything I can think to write. I will draw the details of the animal, the sinus and the tissue as they are torn or cut. I am racing against the inevitable destruction of this animal. I must take care to document every inch, every aspect of its body. I worry, while sweat is in my eyes and my fingers tense, that I will do something wrong, that a crucial element will be missing and this puzzle will never be assembled.*

1879–1887

THE AMERICAN CARNIVAL

*I have butchered many men. All are innocent and
equaled when they are on the table. All are exquisite
and grotesque.*
—Dr. Spencer Black

After concluding his work on the fawn-child, Black decided to publish his findings. He believed that publishing was the only practical, bold, and useful employment of his efforts. Yet, he knew his unorthodox claims would be likely to doom both his future and his reputation as a traditional physician. Despite the risk, Black submitted his findings to the Academy of Medicine. He wrote a comprehensive article outlining his belief that the mutation present in the fawn-child demonstrated proof that the mythological creature known as the satyr was once real, as was evidenced in the body of the fawn-child specimen. The academy rejected his paper.

Black approached twelve other universities located in cities including Chicago, Boston, New York, and London; all met his enthusiasm with rejection.

Within a short time, the Academy of Medicine terminated all funding to Dr. Black. It was clear to his colleagues that Black no longer considered his previous endeavors to be important; he was focused exclusively on his work with the fawn-child. His reputation in the scientific community was falling quickly—he was berated in the press, heckled in the streets, and attacked in personal correspondence.

*Dr. Black's findings are like the far-fetched and fantastic dreams of
a child, not the ideas of a modern scientist.... His claims ought to
be written in a novel, where the audience is more prone to delight
in the hysterics derived from monsters.*

—*Dr. Joab A. Holace*

The damage to Black's reputation was irrevocable. He began accruing debts, but with no hope of professional redemption, he continued his research. As determined as ever, he believed that he would uncover the greatest anthropological discovery of all time.

In 1880, Black joined the American Carnival. At the time, hundreds of carnivals and circuses traveled throughout the United States and the continent of Europe. The American Carnival was not one of the larger traveling shows: with just fifteen horse-drawn caravans, its size was relatively modest. Dr. Black's Anatomical Museum would be a new addition to the carnival—an exhibit consisting of artifacts, specimens, and information that Black had collected through the years.

Black displayed skeletons of real deformities accompanied by an analysis explaining why the bones were malformed. Some of the specimens were laid out on tables; others were displayed in cases, and smaller artifacts were hung from the rafters of the tent. To enhance the show's entertainment value, Black was encouraged to tell stories explaining how his specimens had descended from ancient mythological animals. An excerpt from a flier reads: "A child born without arms may be a confused body that lacked the information to produce wings, of a harpy perhaps."

The transition from esteemed medical prodigy to carnival sideshow host came abruptly for Dr. Black. He and his family were forced to adapt to a new lifestyle, one that was incredibly different from what they had previously been accustomed to. Traveling with a carnival was a considerable hardship, but his wife and sons adapted fairly well. We know that Elise hailed from a prosperous and educated family; she could have easily taken the children to live with her parents and siblings in Chicago. Instead, she became an integral element in the culture of the American Carnival. She was well known among other workers and was well liked, too. By assuming a matronly role as a caregiver to the other performers, she soon earned the nickname "Momma El."

Black's own experience was more complicated. These two journal entries, written just four months apart, illustrate his evolving views concerning his research and the carnival lifestyle.

September 1880

I have devoted my efforts thus far to the fulfillment of my work, only to share it now with liars, criminals, and killers: ignorant people whose only reluctance to eat one another is that they do not care for the taste. Yes, I am in good company, indeed. I entertain the whims of this carnival. I lecture to common citizens less interested in my science than in the so-called lizard-woman from the jungle—who is really only a woman from Detroit afflicted with ichthyosis. It would be more auspicious to work alone in a laboratory, in a university; I could then speak to a dedicated audience of students.

I know I must continue my work, despite my disdain of my audience. Without another source of subsistence I am left with only this one choice.

* * *

February 1881

I can reach out through the boundaries of this country and seek out the ones who will listen as I once did. I am not confined to one state or province; I can take my work to them if they will not come to me. I will appear on their steps and knock on their doors.

Despite an initial hesitation, Black became a phenomenally successful showman, and he soon grew to embrace the fair lifestyle. Among carnival personalities, his style of showmanship was greatly admired. Curious onlookers would flock to the traveling museum, eager to see the controversial exhibits that were contested so vehemently in local newspapers. Profits from the museum were substantial. Black had no trouble providing for his family; he even purchased a decent-sized horse-drawn caravan, the transportation mode of choice for early American carnival and circus professionals. The added mobility allowed him to travel more freely, especially in winter, when the carnival closed.

Gregarious and outspoken, Dr. Black often challenged doubters in the audience to join him in open debate. On one such occasion, in Marris County, New York, in 1881, a minister by the name of William Cathaway Jr. criticized the show's moral decency and blasphemous content. Cathaway was particularly upset by Black's claim that man once existed in a form substantially different from the Old Testament's Adam and Eve.

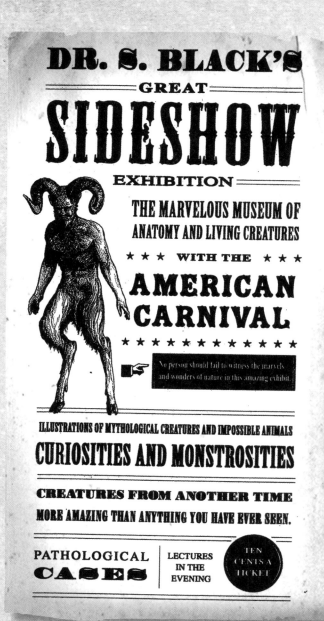

This advertisement for the American Carnival highlights Dr. Black as the main attraction, but in truth he was only a small part of a much larger show. This kind of exaggeration was typical among carnival showmen and suggests that the advertisement was created by Dr. Black himself.

As minister and scientist continued their debate, members of the audience began taking sides, and the confrontation climaxed in a brawl. Both men were arrested, but only Black was charged with inciting a riot. He was not convicted. As a result of this incident, he would spend the next few years enduring constant harassment and arrests, for local authorities believed him to be a nuisance to the common peace. Driven from towns, Black remained unaffected by the persecution. Although never convicted, he was charged with dozens of crimes: larceny, fraud, and public indecency (i.e., placing indecent objects/ scenes or portrayals thereof before the public view), among many others.

> *More effort has been given to prevent the occasion of listening to me than would have been required to simply stand idle while I spoke. Can a scientist truly incite this kind of fear?*

Black soon understood that no amount of intelligent scientific argument was likely to persuade his audience. He needed evidence, and he would have to create it himself. He theorized that the same reasoning used to heal or reverse a deformity could also serve to engineer a deformity; he would have to create what he thought the body (nature) had originally intended.

Black disappeared from the public view for the next few months as he reinvented his show. He undertook his work in the secluded privacy of his carnival caravan. He started with small dead animals and grafted parts of them together, assembling his vision of what the creatures might have looked like. During the summer of 1882, with the help of his five-year-old son Alphonse, Black made frequent trips in search of small game. When the small hunting party found success, father and son would take their quarry into the caravan, nestled in a meadow forty miles north of Philadelphia, and cut the animals' bodies into pieces. On one occasion Black assembled some of these components into a sort of doll that resembled a small harpy. The lower portion consisted of a turkey; soft feathers covered its tough and bare-skinned neck. On top was the head of a small child, which Dr. Black taken from a cadaver. He called the creature Eve.

Eve was followed by a series of even more elaborate creations. Having knowledge of the physiological and anatomical design of living things, Black set out to engineer what he thought was intended by nature to still exist. And so in the year 1883 he built and designed a miraculous cabinet of curiosities—taxidermied replicas of a host of mythological creatures. Any human components involved in the creation of these oddities were likely exhumed from cemeteries by the doctor and Alphonse.

Black presented his revamped museum in the spring of 1884, touring the country with Elise and their two children. Despite his continued difficulty with local police, the show was a tremendous success:

May 9, 1883
They were gathering in crowds like swarms of pests,
murmuring and confused. Suspicious shadows cast over their faces
gave an eerie countenance to all who looked upon my work and
believed in what they saw. They saw the vestige of life's history.

The show was met by enthusiastic and oftentimes frightened or angry audiences. One review states: "It was quite a disturbing thing to see the taxidermy medley of Dr. Black. The animals appeared real, as though their eyes could have opened. All they needed was a nudge and they'd wake up."

Initially, the show included only a small harpy, a Cerberus (a three-headed hell hound), and an Eastern dragon. But audience sensibilities were tested when Black presented a centaur that combined a human cadaver and a dead horse. The macabre scene was simply too grotesque, and audiences protested in horror. A local Philadelphia newspaper wrote, "Dr. Black is still disgusting and lacking the decency, manners, and good sense he once had."

But Black was determined to persevere. He never lost his conviction that all the fantastic creatures he presented were once real. He argued it was his responsibility to science, medicine, and the world to uncover the true nature of man. According to his claims, there once lived more bizarre and unknown creatures in the world than what had been discovered. He believed mermaids once swam in the deep, minotaurs ruled in the hills of Macedonia, and sphinxes nested in the rocks of Mount St. Catherine in Egypt.

Black claimed to have proof of these ancient species, which had been shipped to him from around the world, packed neatly in a case in his caravan. Although it was true he had received many shipments, the contents of those crates are believed to have been specimens of mutations, more oddities for his research from when he was still working in Ward C. Among the objects recovered from the museum was a large crate bearing a bill of lading. It indicated that the parcel had arrived from Constantinople; the shipper's name was illegible. The contents of the crate were unknown, but it was large enough to comfortably fit two adult humans. Unfortunately, even an approximate number of shipments received by Dr. Black remains unknown.

> *Finally, finally it has arrived. I have waited long enough. It feels as though I waited impatiently for a longer time than it took to travel here.*

As Black's popularity grew, increasing numbers of people came to be aware of his unique scientific views as well as those of his critics. It's fair to say that the whole affair turned into a sport with two opposing teams. None of the mania dissuaded Black from remaining in the public eye; in fact, he would often attend social functions, dinners, and public events or political rallies (usually uninvited) specifically to discuss his position and philosophy. It was reported that at a small and exclusive dinner club in New Jersey, Black incited the hostilities of the host when he hurled a glass through a window, attempting to illustrate that God does not intend for man to fly, but man alone intends it. His actions prompted further violence, and the main dining room was destroyed as a result.

> *I hear them marvel at my work—my indignant science. I hear them call out in fear of what they see. And there are some gentlemen who doubt what I tell them. They call me a liar and a charlatan or a quack. But in time the methods of science that I now employ to convince people will surely set them free—alas, this I cannot explain to the angry fools.*

Black had little to no respect for his critics; toward the end of his public career he was known for his volatile behavior and unpredictable personality. As his audience continued to grow, so, too, did his critics. Black worried he wasn't being taken seriously enough; he was a scientist, not an entertainer. Disappointed, he performed only twice in the fall of 1884 before stopping the show and ending his arrangement with the American Carnival. From an article published in a Philadelphia medical journal in July 1884:

> *... He would show ordinary bones from excavations, ordinary remains of a goat or a lion, and tell us that he had discovered evidence of the Sphinx; he lectured endlessly, poring over the smallest details in the bone, revealing its secrets, secrets I could*

never see—none of us could. Now he travels like a common charlatan, displaying his dolls and trinkets as proof. If I stitch together a monster, does that prove its existence? Dr. Spencer Black is a ranting lunatic; he is never content, he continues to see things that do not exist. When a falsehood is coveted long enough, it becomes the truth that sustains its own existence. He is a madman!
—Dr. Joab A. Holace

In late 1884 Black famously delivered this response:

Dr. Holace,

I have delayed the writing of this letter. I know that I am no longer in your favor. I was surprised to hear that you have championed the destruction of my reputation and are unflinching, unrelenting and merciless in your opinion of me.

My dear Doctor, it isn't I who is fanciful and lacking the courage to lay my sights on the true and determined path of thought—but instead, it seems, it is you who is unable and, moreover, unwilling to be ardent in the knowledge that you know not.

I gave you an opportunity to see beyond yourself, beyond your small world and science. I gave you a chance to participate in the greatest anthropological breakthrough any surgeon could have ever dreamed. It is with elation for the preservation of my work and sorrow for the loss of what was once a great friendship that I say farewell to you.

—Spencer Black

On May 3, 1884, Spencer and Elise had a healthy baby boy named Samuel. But the joy of his arrival was cut short by tragedy; their second child, Victor, fell ill for several weeks and died of typhoid fever just four months after Samuel was born. Spencer writes about the event in his journals, dated September 1884:

My dear sweet angel, my dear sweet ... Now he is passed on with his sister, Elizabeth. I, his governor, his father, could not stop him from going; what will come of my other children? Will I be as helpless, when they fall ill? With all that I have labored, and the proficiency that I've gained with my toil, with all the knowledge that I have acquired—measurably more than an ordinary learned man—can I not save my own children? I may just as well kill with my own hands.

Can I only bear witness to death? Can I not share in the glory of life?

Unhappy with the success of the anatomy show and grieving the loss of his son Victor, Black escalated the intensity of his work. He now believed the only way to prove his claims was to make *living* evidence, animated creatures, so that the world could understand.

Immediately after returning home to Philadelphia in the winter of 1884, he began work on grafting living tissue in a small storage shed in the woods behind his home; this shed eventually grew into a sort of laboratory. Black lived in the main house, but every morning he would ride his horse into the woods to continue his work in his lab. He had become obstinately difficult and single-minded regarding his obsession with creating life.

When death arrives, the very life inside of you knows its own fate; it writhes and claws with a ferocity that has no equal. Then in a quick moment, there is no more pain and you can hear the sound of death. She travels to you gently, as though water had been suspended in the air in-between. The sound of her voice greets you with a messenger's reverence and a diplomat's neutrality so that you might be soothed by her meaning and calmed by her presence.

During the next two years Black acquired several small, living animals with which to begin his experiments. His obsession caused him to become estranged from his children and his wife. He struggled greatly with his work and endured many failures in his efforts. After a year and a half, the stress of his conduct was too much for Elise to bear. She wrote to her brother-in-law Bernard, asking him to come to the house:

... dead animals, bloody animals living in cages, dying or soon to be dead, or worse. There's a foul stench that attracts beasts from all over the countryside only to be captured or slain by my husband ... I pray God your brother is well. You ought to pray also ...

In the fall of 1887, Bernard returned to help Elise. Like her, he was greatly concerned about his brother's health and sanity. Spencer Black was reserved, reluctant to talk, and clearly unable to stop working; he would spend entire days alone in his laboratory.

It was in late November 1887, more than a year after the last tour of the carnival show, that Black asked Elise and Bernard to bear witness to the scientific achievement he called a modern renaissance. Neither Elise nor Bernard could have expected what they were about to see. Samuel and Alphonse were with Elise when they entered Black's laboratory; the boys were only about four and sixteen years old. In his journal Bernard describes the scene and the events that followed:

> *My heart turned foul and my skin tightened the length of my body when I saw what my God-damned brother had done. The room was entirely dark except for a small lamp on his desk. Illuminated were pages of notes, jars filled with liquid and pieces of flesh, small empty cages on the floor beside the desk and filth everywhere. The building was dank and smelled of death and excrement. Spencer escorted us closer to his desk where I could see what he was so proud to present. There on the ground was a bleeding animal; a dog with the wings of a rooster sewn onto its back. The animal moved slightly as it breathed, the only evidence that it was alive, though it seemed impossible. It was so disfigured, swollen, and injured. Elise had buried Samuel deep in the folds of her dress with her left arm while her other searched loosely for Alphonse; her eyes were intent on Spencer. She had only looked at the poor animal once, a quick look. She cried, Alphonse stood still, just out of his mother's reach and wearing no expression. The animal flinched in response to Spencer's voice; its wings flapped as it tried to stand. Spencer laughed and clapped his hands together.*
>
> *From the unlit shadows, further back in his lab, came a loud groan and then a crash inside a cage. It was then that we were aware that the poor beast on the ground was not the only animal. Elise ran outside pulling Samuel out with her. She tried to take Alphonse, but he refused, strong enough to wrest free of his mother's grasp. She left him but I did not; I grabbed the wicked boy and commanded that he go to his mother.*
>
> *Once alone with Spencer I screamed in anger, demanding to know: What had he done? What was he doing? I was angry*

with him, angry that he had performed such a cruel act. I did not know how he had achieved such a stunt. He told me that what he had done was clear enough, so clear that the bloody animal on the ground could nearly speak for itself and tell me what had occurred. As Spencer spoke the animal moved frantically. I told him it was dying. I nearly wept as I spoke, I was so overcome. I tried not to look at the creature; its claws scratched along the floor as each attempt to right itself failed. Its body excreted blood and bile from several places; it writhed at Spencer's feet, but he paid his longtime pet no heed as he talked. He explained to me that it was not dying but, rather, living: it was being born. I began to protest his logic but then he screamed so ruthlessly I would have thought he wished me killed. Spencer said that his work was not for me, or for him, but was instead in and of itself a new species, a new science, a new world. He stood in front of the animal, as though he was protecting it. I knew there was nothing I could say to persuade him or calm his anger. I protested one last time.

He spat his words at me, condemning what he called the judiciary of morality and the imperious kings of good works. When he finished, he remained still. The lamplight directly behind him cast a shadow on his face, and though I could not see his eyes, I knew they were on me. I left. I remember those events perfectly, I can still hear his voice. I have not seen him since that day.

There is none who possess that healing power. Spencer holds it gently in his hand as though it were the knowledge of science itself, a living creature that he cradles and carries with him always—like a pet.

Bernard's journal goes on to explain that Elise gave her boys to Bernard and asked him to leave that night, which he did. She told him that she needed to gather some things first and would leave soon after.

Bernard returned to New York, believing there was nothing more he could do for his deeply troubled brother. He tried to take custody of both boys, but Alphonse, then sixteen years old, refused and ran away (returning to the care of his father), and so Bernard arrived in New York with only Samuel, who was nearly four years old at the time.

What Bernard and no one else realized (until the release of Spencer Black's journals many years later) is that Elise returned to the lab on the night of Bernard's departure. Intent on destroying everything her husband had made, she smashed an oil lamp onto his desk, igniting a fire. She then began to shoot his animals with a small pistol. Spencer, hearing the gunshots and seeing the flames from the house, rushed to stop the blaze. Black described the confrontation in his journal:

> I raced across the field, desperate to save my work. I dismounted from my horse with such haste that I nearly did myself in at that moment. I rushed inside and was greeted, without warning, by my Elise and her pistol. She fired and struck me in the leg. I know she had intended to strike my chest. It is fortunate for me that she didn't aim for the ceiling, for then I would certainly be dead. Elise then shot my dog and, after it was killed, continued throughout the burning laboratory, killing all of my animals that remained. The conflagration was too intense and Elise was soon engulfed in its flames. I pulled her to safety.

Elise was nearly burned to death: she was blinded, could no longer speak, and was hardly able to move. It is miraculous she did survive, because her chances of dying of an infection were extremely high.

Black told no one of the accident, not even Bernard. When Alphonse returned home (after fleeing from Bernard's custody), father and son took Elise to the caravan deep in the woods to perform an emergency surgery. Black feared that the natural healing process would interfere with the effectiveness of surgical manipulation.

> We brought the caravan north several miles from any home, unhitched the horses and tied them off at a great distance so they would not be disturbed. I prepared to work there in a glen, far removed from everything.
>
> I had to attempt a skin graft; a procedure this complex was not done often and few surgeons have had any success. For two nights we worked, Alphonse and I. He was frightened and unwilling but I offered him no alternative. I was in short supply of anesthesia and what I administered was insufficient. She was in such horrific agony, but there was no alternative.

Our caravan was too far for any to hear; the lights were oppressively dim and she screamed so loud; it was truly awful. Finally, I had to stop. The operation was not going to work.

I still cannot believe what has occurred. That fire was like the whisper of God; it swept through everything, proud and determined, leaving only myself and that poor woman, that poor thing so destroyed in my arms.

The newspapers criticized Black, attributing the fire to his irresponsible character and reckless scientific experiments; no one knew that Elise had been critically injured in the blaze. Black had no choice but to leave Philadelphia and venture where no one knew of the accident. Elise was indefinitely confined to the caravan, and eventually she became dependent on opium.

1888–1908

THE HUMAN RENAISSANCE

*My lab is more than a cold table fashioned of wood
and metal; it is a heartbeat, a vessel, my home and
temple.*
—Spencer Black

In spite of this family tragedy, Black had reaffirmed his conviction in his work. His journal reveals his feelings after parting company with Bernard, Samuel, and his hometown of Philadelphia.

April 30, 1888

We are now traveling to Chicago; Elise is resting quietly. My brother and I are at odds; our friendship, I fear, is irreconcilable. I had no opportunity to explain myself as well as perhaps he would have required to merit compassion. There was no opportunity, but how could I have? Would I discuss the minutia of the scientific details pertaining to the complex structures of all that governs life and the obedience required to deviate from it? Creating a new specimen? It would require a millennium to explain and write it down. But all the while the creature lived—is that not enough?

I cannot be still, I cannot rest or sleep. I won't escape what I set out to do. My work is more than a curiosity now. I knew nothing when I was young; I was far from death, I couldn't taste it on my teeth as I do now. I didn't give enough thought to what I was doing as a doctor or scientist. I am careful now; I have left whence I came.

*We have finally arrived. It is now morning. I am delighted at
the stillness of the tall grass in the fields and the quiet of the horses,
stopped, steaming with heat and unable to go anymore. Elise is still
asleep; I won't wake her, she had just begun to rest. My beloved
and eternally precious Elise—I could write that a thousand times
and not tire; how it pains me that of all the flowers to bloom this
Spring, she is the one I will not see.*

Upon arriving in Chicago, Black began work on a new show, the Human
Renaissance, that would be a showcase for his living evidence. In 1890, after two years
of development, Black unveiled the show in Boston. Promotional handbills advertised
"The Winged Woman" or "Angel Child," "The Snake Maiden," "The Fire Demon," and
"Darwin's Beagle," a canine with functional wings grafted onto its back.

Some speculated that the creatures were accidental mutations, optical illusions, or
elaborately costumed animals. Others (correctly) believed they were surgically assembled
hybrids. But Dr. Black himself claimed they were newly discovered life forms. From the
fall 1891 issue of *Chicago Journal of Science*:

> *A man, scientist or not, who can manipulate nature through
> vivisection or any means to this end does not practice science
> but instead knows it—and possesses a power that no man should
> wield, for this work no man should have wrought.*
> —*William J. Getty, M.D., F.R.S.C.*
> *(Professor of Surgery in the Anatomy Department of the
> University of Medical Science, New York)*

Some of the performers in the Human Renaissance were Dr. Black's patients from
Ward C; others were patients he'd met during his travels with the American Carnival.
All their conditions were extreme. One young man was said to have had leg transplants;
he bore the limbs of a much taller man with a darker complexion. Another patient was
a formerly conjoined twin, a seventeen-year-old girl named Rose. Her surgical procedure
was so elaborate that it involved a new heart, lung, kidney, spleen, and arm. The girl's
parents said that Black had even made her prettier than before. Her twin sister had died
during the surgery.

To the malformed, the sick, or the diseased, Dr. Black had become something of a

THE
NATIONAL JOURNAL OF MEDICINE AND SCIENCE

VOL. 2 NO. 8   PHILADELPHIA, PA. SEPTEMBER, 1891   EST. 1812

New sideshow at traveling carnival. Medical marvel or menace?

Dr. Spencer Edward Black hosts what he calls, "A triumph over the fate of man," in his traveling sideshow with the American Carnival titled, The Human Renaissance. In this performance he showcases the common thrills that are expected at these events: bizarre skeletons, strange creatures in glass jars, and amputated limbs from a variety of imagined animals among many other odd items. What is most interesting, or disturbing to one's senses, is the taxidermy collection of mythical animals such as: the mermaid, the sphinx, the minotaur, and even a pegasus. It is obvious that these are not real creatures, the doctor will tell you so himself; they are instead, "A vision of what may come." Dr. Black purports that the alleged creatures were once real, and can be made to be real again. Yes it's true, an outlandish claim indeed; however, his presentation has lead to a great deal of trouble for him. Angry mobs gather to protest his work, police are reported to have arrested the doctor on a number of occasions, and it is said that he is even estranged from his own family- all but his son who assists him while on the stage.

The Human Renaissance show will be performing in Philadelphia, October 13-25, and though there are many who are curious, there are many more who are outraged. "Why must he come here with that deplorable act, we are a good city with good sensibilities- we have no need for any of that frankenstein nonsense," says, community organizer, Garth Dewint.

Among the attractions of the sideshow must be included Dr. Spencer Black's most impressive and disconcerting exhibit, Darwin's Beagle.

DR. S. BLACK'S DARWIN'S BEAGLE!

NEW EXHIBITION

ALIVE!

lectures about this amazing creation in the evening

TEN CENTS A TICKET

Pictured above, an event attraction cleverly named, Darwin's Beagle. Only one of many grotesque animals in Dr. Black's cabinet of curiosity.

It is what appears to be an ordinary beagle with working wings; wings that function so well, the animal needs to be chained to the stage so it doesn't fly away from the patrons. If this is indeed an illusion, which it must certainly be, then a splendid one it is. This novelty is a new act for the doctor, and is anticipated to attract a great number of curious onlookers.

-Article written by: David O'Boyle

Local community man complains of rare skin condition

Local man, George J. Spleate, was under the care of Physician Jaques De'van complaining of an irritation and greenish colored rash on the entire surface of his chest.

Newspaper clipping from the *National Journal of Medicine and Science*. Despite their claims of being a national publication, the *Journal* was based in Philadelphia and rarely covered events outside the immediate region. Its readership consisted largely of local residents, not medical professionals.

folk hero. He was ridiculed in the mainstream scientific community but revered by many, especially those afflicted with unusual illnesses. Black wrote this quip to the *Chicago Journal of Science*:

> *Your suspicions are acute and undoubtedly not without the prerequisite research on the nature of my work. Why, you'd think that we [doctors] were monsters the way some go on about their God and sanctimony and blasphemes. We are scientists, not demons.*

The tradition of carnival performers providing food, medicine, and other charities to the needy and sick still carries on in Black's name in many regions of the world. While he toured, his reputation for offering surgical help, sometimes called miracles, was widespread enough to warrant pilgrimages to see him. There are accounts of children suffering from life-threatening defects whose families traveled hundreds of miles, and sometimes even farther, to seek out his services. On one such occasion Black wrote in October 1891:

> *She was brought to us with neither arms nor legs, brought not only to our show, but here on Celestial Terra itself. When she was found, there were none to claim her. She was alone save the box and a letter that the poor child was abandoned with. Her family, ashamed of their daughter, failed to see what she really was—they saw only a monster. The condition of her birth and deformity was not a punishment or an omen or a hex cast upon her. She has lost blood, precious blood. I will give her back what was supposed to be hers.*

The patient was a nine-year-old girl, Miriam Helmer. She was born with no arms (only hands) and very short legs, quite possibly a form of the condition known as Roberts syndrome. Dr. Black grafted wings onto the girl's shoulders, and, after a brief healing period, she began performing in his show. Black presented her as the winged woman, claiming that her lack of arms was a genetic attempt to sprout wings; the failure could be attributed to the fact that her composition was largely human. Miriam performed in the show for several years before she died from unknown causes in 1899.

With Miriam Helmer, Black introduced his theory of self-resurrection—the idea that he could unlock the body's natural memory of its ancestral past by giving it real physical reminders. Armed with these prompts, the body could rebuild on its ancient knowledge and then "self-resurrect." He cites numerous references to self-resurrection in a book called *The Book of Breath*, but it is widely believed this book is one that Black himself was writing. To this day, no manuscript or volume with a similar title or description has ever been found.

The Human Renaissance show ran from 1892 to 1893 and attracted controversy with every new performance. Disturbances and fights were common, religious leaders protested Dr. Black's creations, political leaders spoke out against him, and nearly the entire medical community decried his legitimacy. Even the American Eugenics Society found fault with Dr. Black, describing his work as regressive:

> *[It is] an abolition of modern efforts—an attack on the human form. These beasts are not natural, as Dr. Black says. They ought not be displayed for the public but rather driven back into extinction.*
> —*Edward Stalts, Director of the American Eugenics Society*

But as has been evidenced all along, Black was not easily discouraged; he was accustomed to arguing and fighting. He had grown into a different kind of showman, one who was quick-tempered and eager to rouse a crowd into a frenzy. His last public performance was at the 1893 World's Columbian Exposition in Chicago. Scheduled to perform for two months, he lasted just three days. At every show, he was mocked and ridiculed; the mobs grew larger and larger. On the third day of performances, the crowd rushed his stage, killed some of the animals, and burned many of his artifacts before forcing him out. Black was devastated.

July 1893

Bernard,

Perhaps you have heard, perhaps the jubilant laughter of my demise was carried freely through the air by Hermes himself, or perhaps you still do not know. I was in attendance at the Columbian Exposition—The World's Fair. I was ridiculed, mocked, and spit upon. They meant to harm me. These are the people, the public, whom I as a doctor ventured to heal? These are the wounded and sick that I labored to discover cures and remedies for?

What wretched flesh they are. They will learn that I can do much more than heal, dear brother—I swear to you that. I can do much more now.

Your brother—do not forget that.

After his failure in Chicago, Dr. Black would never host another public appearance, although he would continue to perform in private for select audiences. These shows were not widely advertised (and in most cases were not publicized at all). There is little information about the contents of the guest list or what exactly the performances entailed. Itineraries suggest that the show remained active, visiting three or four venues every week.

We do believe that the show remained in cities for only one or two days at a time. Sometimes it was presented in private homes or theaters; often Dr. Black had no choice but to perform in secluded wilderness settings. It's rumored that he performed in the Hills Capital Building in Harrisburg, Pennsylvania, just one night before it was burned to the ground. In various journals and diaries, spectators have described an "unholy" feeling about the performance and its practitioners.

The show traveled in America until the winter of 1895. Spencer, Elise, Alphonse, and possibly six or more performers and assistants were leaving New York, but instead of heading south to avoid the coming cold weather, Black decided to travel north to meet with Alexander Goethe. Goethe was a wealthy, eccentric naturalist who paid Black for a private demonstration of the show, to be performed at his opulent palatial estate.

Goethe possessed several bizarre "cabinets of curiosities," which were common among aristocrats of the late nineteenth century. The care and effort given to his collection were extraordinary; it was often described as "a new wonder of the world." There were so many artifacts that they required their own separate building: dried skins of Visigoth warriors, Mayan weapons, embalmed priests from Egypt, and a number of questionable artifacts, including the arm of a siren and the torso of a sphinx. Goethe claimed that he fished the arm of the siren from the Indian Ocean and said that it fought with a ferocity that made him believe he had hooked a Spartan soldier instead. He claimed that the sphinx was found dead on the shore of the Nile and beasts had torn it to pieces, leaving only the tattered remains that he housed in his museum.

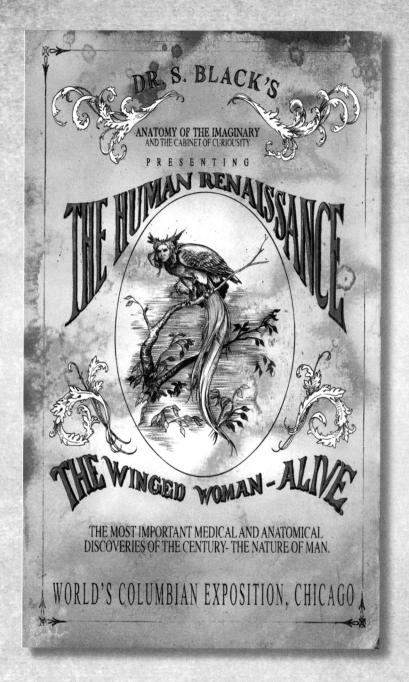

Advertisement for the World's Columbian Exposition, also known as the World's Fair, 1893. The bird-faced creature (harpy) in the center was possibly one of Black's earlier taxidermy creations. One spectator claimed, "We saw the beasts move on the stage. They crowed and moaned like real living things. Not God's creatures but instead something else, something terrible." Many dismissed the performance as a type of hoax or optical illusion.

Spring 1896
A chance encounter has allowed me an introduction to the
well-known Alexander Goethe—explorer, collector of all things,
and man of the world. He was not as I supposed him to be. No, he
was a crass and unpleasant creature, his spine crooked in the side,
his bones too long for his legs and scorn painted on his face.
The man spoke from within a cloud of smoke sweeter than the
scent of opium. He told me he smoked the nectar of the lotus and
that only he knew how to extract the essential ingredients needed
for the everlasting smoke. After a time, I was invited to see his
vast collection, a superior one to any I had ever borne witness to.
Though I swore to him that I would not disclose what was housed
therein, neither in public nor in privately recorded accounts, I can
testify that there are indeed wonders in this world.

No records remain of Goethe's extraordinary collection; most of it was consumed in a 1902 blaze. A few artifacts were recovered, but certainly nothing remarkable. It is likely there was nothing worth recovering, anyway: Alexander Goethe was arrested in 1897 for fraud and theft, and he died in prison in 1912.

At the beginning of the twentieth century, Dr. Black took the Human Renaissance overseas, where it performed quite well. There are accounts of performances in the British Isles, Europe, and farther south in what is now Turkey, Syria, and Israel. Evidence of its presence can be found in nearby museums; the local folklore includes tales of a magician with a magic knife and testimonies from people claiming to have been healed by Dr. Black.

Throughout the international tour, Black claimed he had the power to raise the dead, to make people live longer or even forever. He asserted that he could change the genders and ages of his patients. He performed his surgeries live on stage, in what surely must have been macabre performances. Two descriptions are given here by anonymous spectators:

May 3, 1900
He spoke to the audience for a very long time, discussing
things I didn't really understand but it sounded sensible and I
knew what he meant—but I didn't understand. He then escorted
one of his guests from behind the back of the curtains; the doctor
explained that the man's legs had been amputated after an infection
took over. The doctor's assistants then placed the man on the table.

Dr. Black began to work immediately; remarkably, the man didn't seem to feel any pain. I had seen this sort of thing before, so I thought it was going to be just a trick. There was so much blood though and I was sitting very close; I knew it was real. He took the legs of a dead man and sewed them on. He told us that this procedure can only be done if the body of the donor was recently deceased—very recently, he said. That's when I didn't want to watch any longer but I couldn't leave, the theater was so quiet, how could I have left? ... After only an hour, the man walked. Everyone applauded but I couldn't; how could I? I saw demon magic, on stage, everyone saw it. The devil has his own private surgeon, and I saw him ...

* * *

June 12, 1901

I witnessed this creation with my own cognition, reason, scientific training, and—least of all—my eyes. This was neither nature nor mischief. The creatures deceased and embalmed, were as described on the playbill, but more perfect than I had expected in their proportions and in what appeared to be a natural displacement of all organic systems, hair, muscle, etc. ...

I cannot imagine a feasible method to arrive at the same result if I were charged with the task of creating such a thing. If this was the work of a charlatan or fraud, then perhaps one of either immense skill or supernatural assistance; the latter I reject, the former troubles me as though I had witnessed a magic trick so persuasive that it was not a trick at all. I am unable to understand this thing which I saw laid before God and spectator.

These performances made Spencer Black incredibly wealthy, even as more and more people described him as one of the greatest con men of his time. Critics wrote, "He is nothing more than a magician or a trickster" and "Dr. Black is here to take your money and your good senses." Yet curiously no records exist of any critics who admitted to viewing the show.

It is rumored that Dr. Black performed surgery on his son Alphonse, completing a procedure that rendered him "ageless." He then christened him with a new name, the

Sleepless Man. Black makes reference to this in a passage from his journals:

> *I can prevent death. I can dip my hand into the pool of the fountain of youth; I can cause one to live, be born from death or be spared of its ravages. The sleepless man will forever drink from that fountain. After one sees the true work of God laid beside the work of man for the benefit of comparison, then one can learn finally, as a child does, that the latter is merely a trinket—an object that does nothing.*
>
> *I have come to know that a great number of scientists are atheistic by social ideological comparisons, though they may believe in God, their fundamental belief in nature forbids them from any canonical society. What surprises me greatly is the number of religious surgeons and scientists alike. One can only pretend they do not understand the true meaning of nature for a finite length of time. Their confession is inevitable.*
>
> *It is no man's right to see what I show them—but instead a privilege. This privilege must be bridled by a discretion that only I can discern, that only I am able to judge.*

The show continued for eight years until a private performance in Budapest during the fall of 1901 went terribly wrong. During that show one of his creatures, the Serpent Queen, attacked a member of the audience. Nothing more is known about the performance or the victim. The written accounts by local authorities reveal only that the patron died while in attendance of the performance called the Human Renaissance, hosted by the American surgeon and performer Dr. Spencer Black. The incident must have had a great impact on Black because he never performed again. He returned to his house in Philadelphia, where he proceeded to expand his research facility.

Since leaving Spencer and taking custody of Samuel in 1887, Bernard Black had remained in New York, where he met and married Emma Werstone, a wealthy widow from a good family. Her first husband, an officer in the southern frontier, had been killed in the Spanish–American War. Bernard and Emma were married in 1899 and together they raised Samuel, a promising student interested in architecture and engineering. He went on to graduate from the prestigious Wayne and Miller School of Architecture.

As the Human Renaissance traveled throughout Europe, Bernard received numerous letters from Spencer. Most were short, incomplete, and often frightfully obscure and confusing. Because Spencer was always moving from one town to the next, there was no way for Bernard to deliver a reply. This may explain why Spencer's letters often read like journal entries or inebriated nonsense. Strangely, he never mentions Elise's horrible condition; his letters to Bernard suggest that they are merely suffering from domestic troubles.

December 1897

Dearest Brother,

All things are unrelenting; all of the once gentle and supple nectars of life are now venomous and cruel. I am unable to manage my affairs. My bones have dried and cracked and my poor Elise doesn't forgive me ... I know what she must think of me. My son, Alphonse is a beast of another sort—he is often angry, he has a deep internal malady, I fear him ... his destiny.

I have nothing now. I am tired and care little of anything. I am lost, dear brother.

I miss the company you had once offered. I regret that I cannot see you and I do wish—most sincerely—that you are filled with joy, that life cradles you as one of its most beloved.

Spencer

* * *

June 1898

Dear friend Bernard,

I trust this letter finds you well. It has been a long while since my last letter. I have been quite busy, I assure you. I cannot say very much at the moment, for the work undertaken and what is presently at hand is far too difficult to detail within the pages of a mere note.

I can say that I offer great apologies to you. I did not mean to cause you alarm or worry at my less orthodox interests. I have suffered a great number of tragedies. My beloved Elise is well; she manages, I suspect.

I will be leaving for a travel excursion that may take a great deal of time to complete.

Your Brother, S.

* * *

August 1900

Bernard,

    I must express my gratitude, insomuch that your foreboding of my certain demise can only attest to your love and most heartfelt concern for me. I had time to consider in depth that which you have instructed me, years ago, regarding what to pay heed to whilst I continue my work further. I trust I will be in your debt and I thank you—though I admit I would be grateful if in matters of peril and premonitions of gloom that you were not a sophist but indeed a fool.

    Dear brother—you preserved your life, you coveted it; it was impossible for you to continue in medicine with sickness and death all around, you needed to pursue a quieter science—I understand.

    You steadily follow the guidance of the learned; you read what you have been instructed to read. You are like a child at practice on a piano. You balance a stick on the backs of your hands just along the knuckles while you play, ensuring proper posture. Then you play something bland and unimaginative; however, the stick will never fall to the floor, bravo! When I perform, the stick falls, then a symphony flows from me.

—Black

* * *

October 1901

Bernard,

    I am no longer performing, or traveling. I now indulge in the luxury and leisure of my home. I am no longer in the service of man.

    You must know these creations can mean nothing to you nor any other educated man as they meant nothing to me until they were there, on a table before me. Their fatal wounds visible, the hollow in their gaze that no taxidermist could create. No artist or magician is able to conjure the sincerity that only life can bring to the eyes. Bernard, I tell you, I now have them. They live.

I understand if you have concerns for my welfare. In time, after my research is complete, I will unveil my discovery. I am as confident as the sun is bright that you won't be disappointed. All is progressing well with little disruption; I pray heaven not change that, I cannot afford a disturbance. My time now is vital, and how long I need I could never know.

I trust that you have, by this point, received the gift I sent to Samuel and I hope that all is in good order with you and my most gifted child. His well-being is certainly my greatest wish, and a promising future I am certain is assured whilst he remains in your steady care.

Please forgive my flattery as I am writing on a rare occasion of delight and rejoicing and all seems wonderful; the only dread, I suppose, is that I am restrained to the primitive exercise of poets and dreamers: scratching on paper, splashing ink, fumbling to communicate my joy, my bliss and exaltation. Finally, Bernard, I have finally come close enough to see that it can be achieved. If I could I wouldn't write another stroke, I would grab hold of you and show you. Against your will and in defiance of your doubts, I would throw you to the floor of my laboratory so that you would gaze up as I did and be prostrate before it as I was and you would marvel as I do now.

Now surely you understand the meaning of my queer gift.

—S. Black

In 1908, Spencer Black entered negotiations with a New York publishing house, Sotsky and Son, for publication of his masterwork, *The Codex Extinct Animalia*. Only six copies were completed before Dr. Black withdrew the project and abruptly disappeared. The reasons for his sudden departure remain unknown.

Dr. Black had garnered many enemies during his career in the sciences, not the least of whom were the administration and colleagues of his former employer, the Academy of Medicine. Dr. Joab Holace, for example, never stopped attacking Black's credibility and legitimacy. His articles were published in many well-known papers: *London's Royal Society of Surgeons Review* in 1891, the *New York Medical Journal* in 1894, 1896, 1897, and again in 1908, with specific mention of Black's book.

Dr. Spencer Quack is going to loft a fairy tale that can barely serve as adequate kindle for the fire. I have not read it, nor do I wish to. I am certain that the ink used to describe the creatures from his own madness is a waste of resources. His book will be nothing more than an extravagant and expensive joke the fool will play on himself.
—Joab A. Holace M.D., N.Y.C.M.
(The N.Y. Medical Journal, 1908)

After 1908, Alphonse continued alone in the strange practices of his father. In 1917, he was caught butchering small animals in a barn twenty-five miles north of Philadelphia; he was arrested and committed to a mental asylum. He remained there for eleven years, receiving only one visitor, in 1920: his younger brother Samuel. In 1929 the building burned down from a fire caused by lightning. During the storm, many of the patients escaped. Alphonse was among them.

From 1933 to 1947 Alphonse allegedly kept a private zoo, where he housed many of his own creations. He inherited his father's fortune and also gained his own tremendous wealth by claiming to be able to restore youth and beauty for an astounding price. Nevertheless, little is known of Alphonse or his work. Like his father, he was extremely secretive.

As for Spencer Black, nothing is known of his whereabouts after 1908. There were no more public appearances; there were no more surgeries. He simply vanished. In 1925, his home in Philadelphia was turned into a small museum, where docents offered tours and lectures explaining his life and work. The museum closed in 1930. The property changed owners several times until 1968, when the last owners suddenly moved out, complaining of strange noises. The building is presently condemned.

The final clue to Dr. Spencer Black's fate is a letter addressed to his brother, Bernard, sent seven years after their last correspondence. It is the last known document written by Black. He had just returned from a six-month excavation and research trip from the northernmost point of Greenland. The letter indicates that he had been actively pursing some bizarre treatment for his wife, Elise. Prior to receiving the letter, Bernard had no knowledge that Elise had been burned in a fire, or that Spencer had performed any kind of surgery on her. Bernard shared the letter with the police before embarking on a trip to find his brother.

February 1908

Bernard,

I have no choice but to conclude the fallacy of my previous studies, however painful it is to accept. I am writing you tonight to give the deepest thanks and offer the most sincere apology a man such as I can manage. Deluded by my own aims, I could not heed your most eloquent and obvious warning. I could not listen well enough to hear that the future of my work had been foretold by the mistakes of my predecessors, men I hadn't the courage to name as mentors ... especially you.

I now languish in the solitude of this letter, lamenting. Your laughter at my expense or your scorn would be a salve upon my mind. Nothing can help me, I know; it was I who was the cause of my peril.

I cannot be certain if you will ever receive this letter, nor is there much I would expect to arise from it if you could read it now. I can be certain, however, that if any news of me arrives to you it will be this letter and this letter alone. I have hidden my notes for you to retrieve. Please, brother, help me keep this from the sleepless man, my son, Alphonse.

I fear you know of what I am to write, but I fervently hope that you do not. I pray that my work, my labor of the past ten years has exceeded any science or philosophy that the learned shall ever endeavor, or be called upon, to examine. If that is so, then perhaps it will end here with me—this box that I have opened. I have succeeded, I have done what none other before me has.

I write only to you. I know that by now I am wretched in your esteem and that you haven't even a decent man's regard for me; I had once hoped that, perhaps, before we were in the grave, we could once again be friends ... I know that cannot be.

My beloved and eternally precious Elise ... how beautiful she was. I did love Elise dearly, but that is not why I ventured to perform this wicked work. I have butchered many men; all are innocent when they are on my table, all are exquisite.

My purpose has exceeded my function, I am afraid. I have spent my life, the vainglory of my youth, consumed and drunken with the most sadistic of all exploits—study. How can one dare travel into the unknown? Something quite terrible is waiting there, a destruction that would not be mine had I not sought after it.

There was a time in the world when nature wore a different mask; since I set out to discover her secrets, my trials have only increased. What struggles, attempting to see that original face, nature's original design. Now destiny has fulfilled her carefully plotted plan, my eventual and total ruin. Now she laughs and I will hear that mother of nature every night until my time arrives; I will hear her calling. That wretch, that filth-soaked thing whose foulness is exceeded only by her demon song.

Death, so terrible an object; you look away from it, fearing that it may see you and call your name. I have seen many die, scream, and many more writhe in anguish at the hands of disease, injury or healing. I am shamed to confess that when a patient screamed I was relieved some—I know their agony was less than what it could have been. But know this: if they knew what horrible things were available to them, they would take comfort in their own suffering.

We are living creatures, and within us is more than we know; the seed of life and death, together. It's sewn into our bodies at birth; it can live and die without us. I have seen it and nurtured it and fought and defended it. I have sacrificed and bled and now I, too, will perish for it, because of it—I know not how to destroy it. I can hear her, that sound—I can hear the screaming—soaring in the darkness, searching for me. I can hear Hell calling my name. Elise, my dear wife! I resolved to save her. I chose to give her a great gift, an ancient past resurrected. She was a descendant of a powerful species, the Fury. Elise is now no longer the same woman, nor is she the one in the cracked body of burned flesh. She has emerged, she has awoken like the cicada.

I learned many things, I wield a mighty sword now. I have taken her, as a worm, an opium-addicted wretch, writhing in a scorched body; listen to me Bernard, I write only truths. She now pounds the air with her wings and bellows Hell's song in hunger. I baptized her; with my knife, I saved her ... again, I saved her.

The last stone I unturned in my quest was the tombstone ... Come quickly.

—S. Black.

Bernard never returned to his wife, Emma, in New York.

In 1908, fifty years after the publication of *Gray's Anatomy*, Dr. Spencer Black arranged for the publication of his *Codex Extinct Animalia*. Just six copies were printed before Dr. Black withdrew the project and disappeared; the book was never distributed, and the Philadelphia Museum of Medical Antiquities has the only known existing copy. Why Dr. Black stopped printing so abruptly (and then vanished) remains unknown.

The book is an anatomical reference manual, a common endeavor among naturalists at the time. It highlights the anatomies of eleven different species that are, as indicated by the title page, proposed to be extinct. At the beginning of each chapter, Dr. Black discusses key points of interest regarding the respective species. Although he sometimes mentions finding specimens (or the partial remains of a specimen) in his travels, it is generally believed that Black fabricated all these creatures by hand. The whereabouts of the specimens remains unknown; most were likely destroyed, but it is possible that some are in the collections of as-yet-unknown individuals.

At times Dr. Black's writing is scattered and difficult to understand. There is a certain hysterical tone to his descriptions that was characteristic of Black in his later years.

THE

CODEX EXTINCT ANIMALIA

A STUDY OF THE LESSER KNOWN SPECIES OF THE ANIMAL KINGDOM

DESIGNED AS A REFERENCE FOR
ALL PRACTITIONERS IN SCIENCE,
MEDICINE, AND PHILOSOPHY

BY

SPENCER EDWARD BLACK, M.D.

WITH

*comprehensive illustrations and explanatory
texts regarding the musculature and skeletal
systems: additional viscera of select animals*

NEW YORK

SOTSKY AND SON

Dr. Black chooses the sphinx for the first chapter, possibly as a reference to her famed riddle. Failure to answer the riddle correctly resulted in instant death. There is, however, nothing enigmatic about Black's intentions. Knowing that most of his specimens would likely be destroyed or hidden away in private collections, he created the codex as a legacy of his research—and, perhaps, as a map for future scientists to follow.

In addition to a brief introduction, each chapter features a stylized drawing—a vision of what Black thought the creatures may have looked like.

SPHINX ALATUS

KINGDOM	*Animalia*	FAMILY	*Felidæ*
PHYLUM	*Vertebrata*	GENUS	*Sphinx*
CLASS	*Echidnæ*	SPECIES	*Sphinx alatus*
ORDER	*Praesidium*		

MANY DETAILS REGARDING the heraldry of the sphinx are still unknown. These creatures varied widely throughout the African continent. In Egypt, there are great statues of this animal—the *sphinx sol*, the protector and scourge of Ra, the sun god. Sphinxes are shown bearing a ram's head (a *criosphinx*) or a goat's head. These species are typically depicted without wings; I suspect that, like many flightless birds, the sphinx lost its need for flight because of geographical isolation. This evolution likely occurred before the animal's arrival in Egypt or Africa; however, I cannot determine whence it originated.

The famed sphinx of Thebes appears strikingly similar to the specimen in my record. Though few in number, the species had a developed human mind with an advanced intellect; they were more than likely fierce and successful predators.

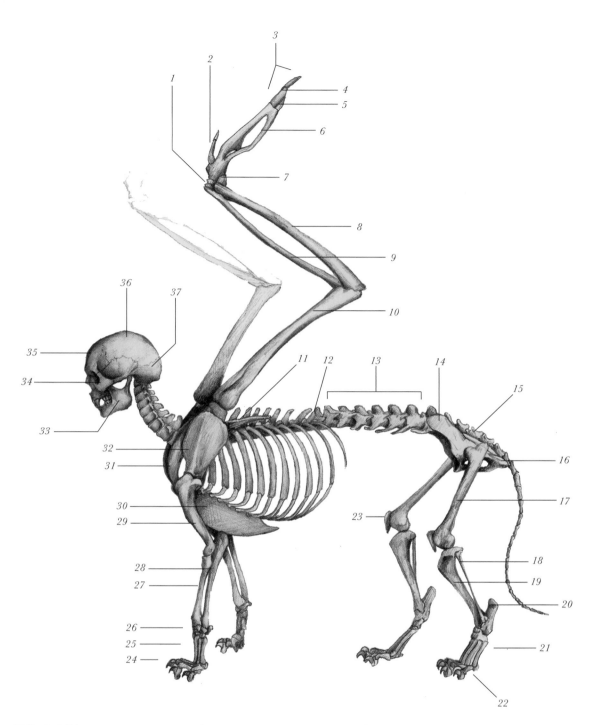

PLATE 1

1- Radial carpal
2- 1st finger
3- Phalanges
4- 2nd finger
5- 3rd finger
6- Carpometacarpus
7- Ulnar carpal
8- Ulna

9- Radius
10- Humerus
11- Scapula
12- 12th thoracic vertebra
13- Lumbar vertebra
14- Pelvis
15- Sacrum
16- Ischial tuber
17- Femur
18- Fibula

19- Tibia
20- Calcanean bone
21- Metatarsal bones
22- Phalanges
23- Patella
24- Phalanges
25- Metacarpal bones
26- Carpal bones
27- Radius
28- Ulna

29- Humerus
30- Keel of sternum
31- Furculum
32- Scapula
33- Mandible
34- Zygomatic arch
35- Frontal bone
36- Parietal bone
37- Occipital bone

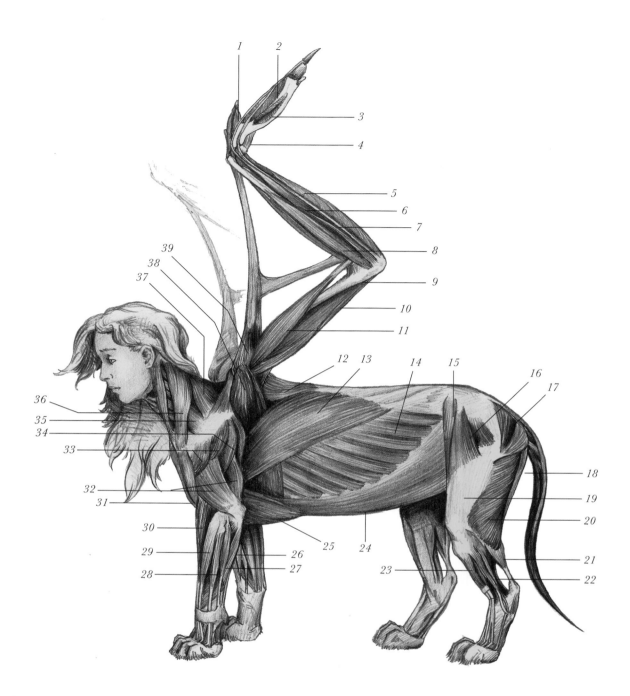

PLATE 2

1- *Adductor alulae*
2- *Adductor digiti majoris*
3- *Interosseus ventralis*
4- *Ulnimetacarpalis dorsalis*
5- *Flexor carpi ulnaris*
6- *Flexor digitorum profundud*
7- *Flexor digitorum superficialis*
8- *Pronator superficialis*
9- *Humerus*
10- *Triceps brachii*
11- *Biceps brachii*
12- *Trapezius*
13- *Latissimus dorsi*
14- *Obliquus externus abdominis*
15- *Sartorius*
16- *Tensor fasciae latae*
17- *Gluteus superficialis*
18- *Semitendinosus*
19- *Quadriceps femoris*
20- *Biceps femoris*
21- *Gastrocnemius*
22- *Flexor digitorum profundus*
23- *Tibialis cranialis*
24- *Vagina recti abdominis*
25- *Pectoralis minor*
26- *Flexor carpi ulnaris*
27- *Extensor carpi ulnaris*
28- *Extensor digitorum lateralis*
29- *Extensor digitorum communis*
30- *Extensor carpi radialis*
31- *Cleidobrachialis*
32- *Triceps brachii*
33- *Deltoideus*
34- *Infraspinatus*
35- *Omotransversarius*
36- *Brachiocephalicus*
37- *Trapezius*
38- *Pectoralis major*
39- *Tensor propatagialis*

SPHINX ALATUS

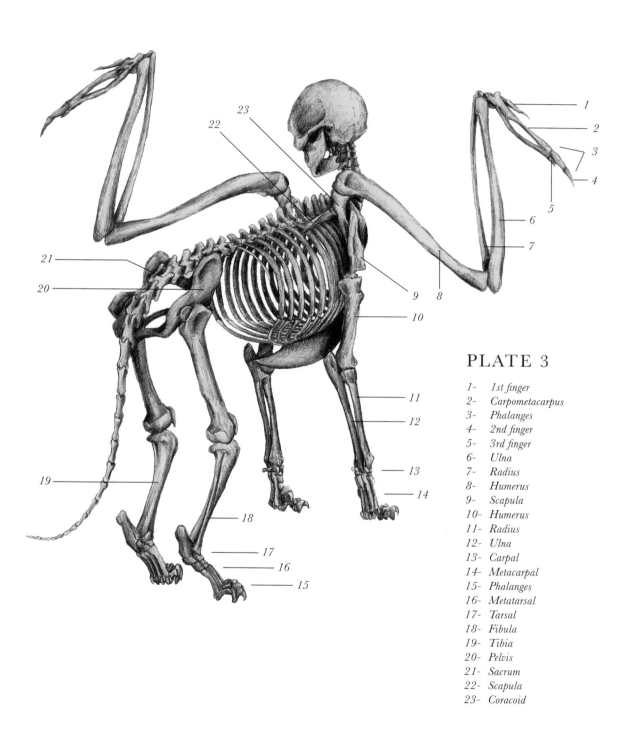

PLATE 3

1- 1st finger
2- Carpometacarpus
3- Phalanges
4- 2nd finger
5- 3rd finger
6- Ulna
7- Radius
8- Humerus
9- Scapula
10- Humerus
11- Radius
12- Ulna
13- Carpal
14- Metacarpal
15- Phalanges
16- Metatarsal
17- Tarsal
18- Fibula
19- Tibia
20- Pelvis
21- Sacrum
22- Scapula
23- Coracoid

SPHINX ALATUS

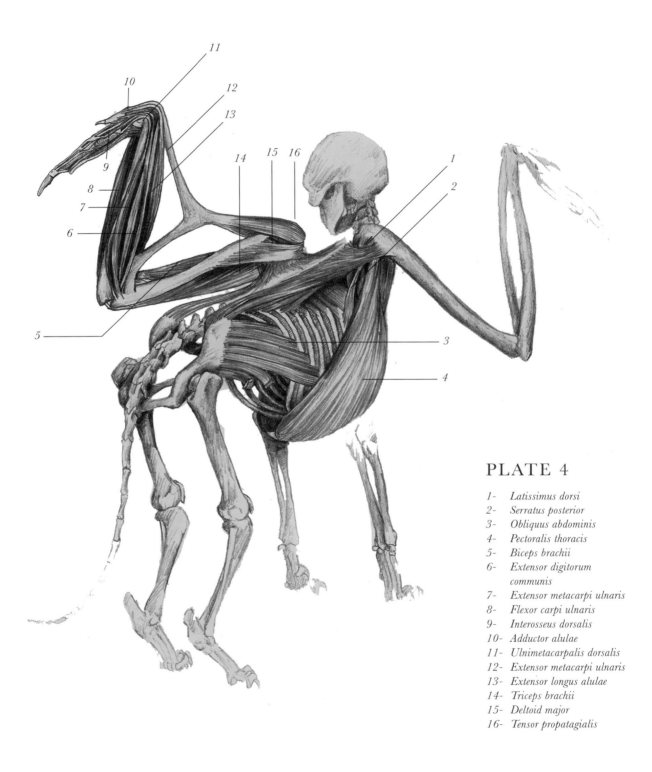

PLATE 4

1- *Latissimus dorsi*
2- *Serratus posterior*
3- *Obliquus abdominis*
4- *Pectoralis thoracis*
5- *Biceps brachii*
6- *Extensor digitorum communis*
7- *Extensor metacarpi ulnaris*
8- *Flexor carpi ulnaris*
9- *Interosseus dorsalis*
10- *Adductor alulae*
11- *Ulnimetacarpalis dorsalis*
12- *Extensor metacarpi ulnaris*
13- *Extensor longus alulae*
14- *Triceps brachii*
15- *Deltoid major*
16- *Tensor propatagialis*

SPHINX ALATUS

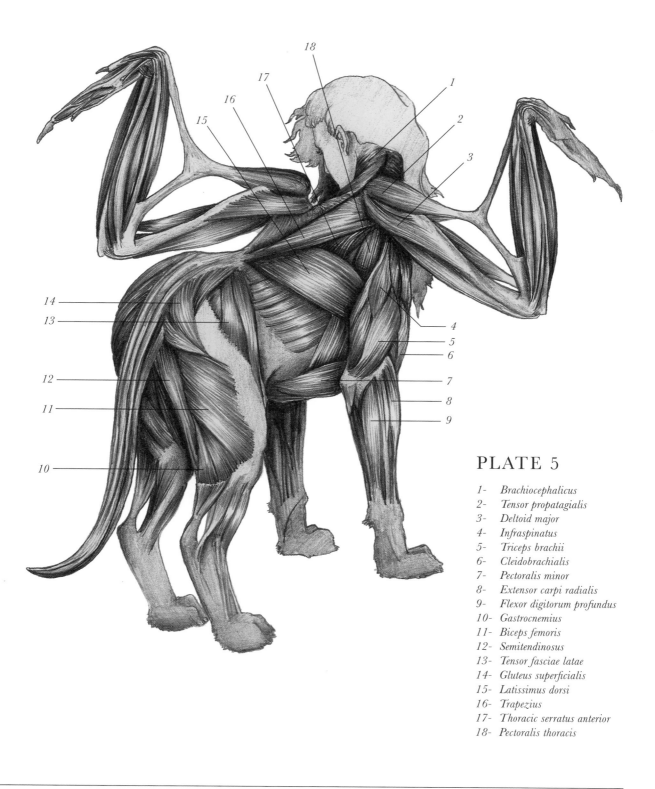

PLATE 5

1- *Brachiocephalicus*
2- *Tensor propatagialis*
3- *Deltoid major*
4- *Infraspinatus*
5- *Triceps brachii*
6- *Cleidobrachialis*
7- *Pectoralis minor*
8- *Extensor carpi radialis*
9- *Flexor digitorum profundus*
10- *Gastrocnemius*
11- *Biceps femoris*
12- *Semitendinosus*
13- *Tensor fasciae latae*
14- *Gluteus superficialis*
15- *Latissimus dorsi*
16- *Trapezius*
17- *Thoracic serratus anterior*
18- *Pectoralis thoracis*

SPHINX ALATUS

75

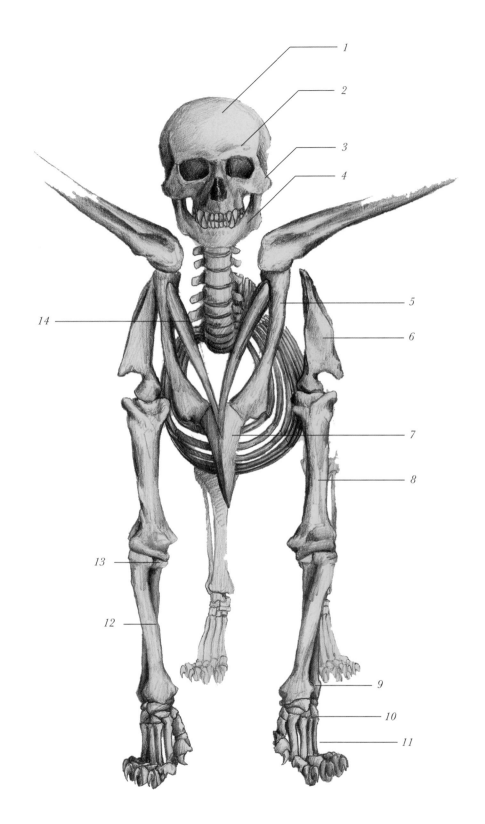

PLATE 6

1- *Frontal bone*
2- *Superciliary crest*
3- *Zygomatic arch*
4- *Mandibula*
5- *Coracoid*
6- *Scapula*
7- *Sternum*
8- *Humerus*
9- *Carpal bones*
10- *Metacarpal bones*
11- *Phalanges*
12- *Radius*
13- *Ulna*
14- *Furculum*

SPHINX ALATUS

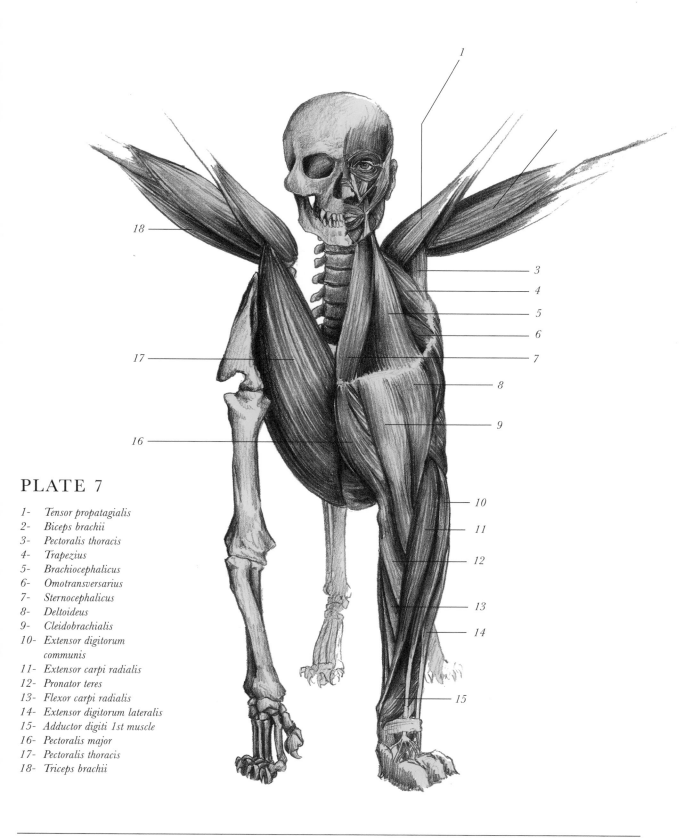

PLATE 7

1- *Tensor propatagialis*
2- *Biceps brachii*
3- *Pectoralis thoracis*
4- *Trapezius*
5- *Brachiocephalicus*
6- *Omotransversarius*
7- *Sternocephalicus*
8- *Deltoideus*
9- *Cleidobrachialis*
10- *Extensor digitorum communis*
11- *Extensor carpi radialis*
12- *Pronator teres*
13- *Flexor carpi radialis*
14- *Extensor digitorum lateralis*
15- *Adductor digiti 1st muscle*
16- *Pectoralis major*
17- *Pectoralis thoracis*
18- *Triceps brachii*

SPHINX ALATUS

The belief in the siren or mermaid was not uncommon in the nineteenth century. Many naturalists and taxonomists maintained that such a creature was plausible. Dr. Black himself states that the oceans were far too vast to reach a decisive conclusion. It is worth noting that, for all the scientists opposed to Black's research, there were many who supported him, and even made similar claims of their own.

SIREN
OCEANUS

KINGDOM	Animalia	FAMILY	Sirenidæ
PHYLUM	Vertebrata	GENUS	Siren
CLASS	Mammichthyes	SPECIES	Siren oceanus
ORDER	Caudata		

THE SIREN, NEREID, AND mermaid are oft confused. The folklore of these creatures predates the conventions of the scientific method; nonetheless, the legends denote an accurate account of some of the evolutionary aspects regarding their species. I will begin with the homogenous nature of them as a species, differing only as dogs may differ in breed— albeit significant differences, indeed.

The siren was described as a bird in ancient times; only later did it become a woman of the water. There was, at some point in the past, a need to make specific distinctions between the water-human and the bird-human animals. Whether it was an error in classification or that the siren evolved into an aquatic mammal is not well understood.

Nereids, or naiades, share many of the traits of the deeper ocean-born species, but they are far more human than the mermaid; and, in many cases, they are nearly entirely human, save the distinct physiological aquatic attributes. This would explain their geographic preference for shallow, fresh water.

The mermaid (the female of the species *Siren oceanus*) was less common and certainly more elusive than the siren. It breathed underwater without any need to surface. I speculate the possibility of several variants of the species that exhibit more mammalian traits and therefore required the occasional breath, as do the dolphin and whale. The task of discovering any such animals intact by means of good fortune alone are nearly impossible.

This animal would need to have a fully evolved and substantially unique respiratory system; similar to the gills of a fish but conforming to the structure of the human rib cage. If my theory is correct and there was once indeed an air-breathing mermaid, this would suggest the existence of a vast variety of species still occupying many shapes, sizes, and functions in the depths of our waters.

The pelvis and femur would be robust and generous in length. Considering the large size of the lumbar vertebrae and the thickness of the caudal and anal spines, this particular species of mermaid would have exhibited a greater agility and speed than nearly any other sea animal hitherto documented. The superficial tendons weave over the muscular tissues, allowing for greater tension, strength, and resistance. The presence of massive muscular tissue supporting all the fin spine regions would grant this animal superiority: a champion in the water.

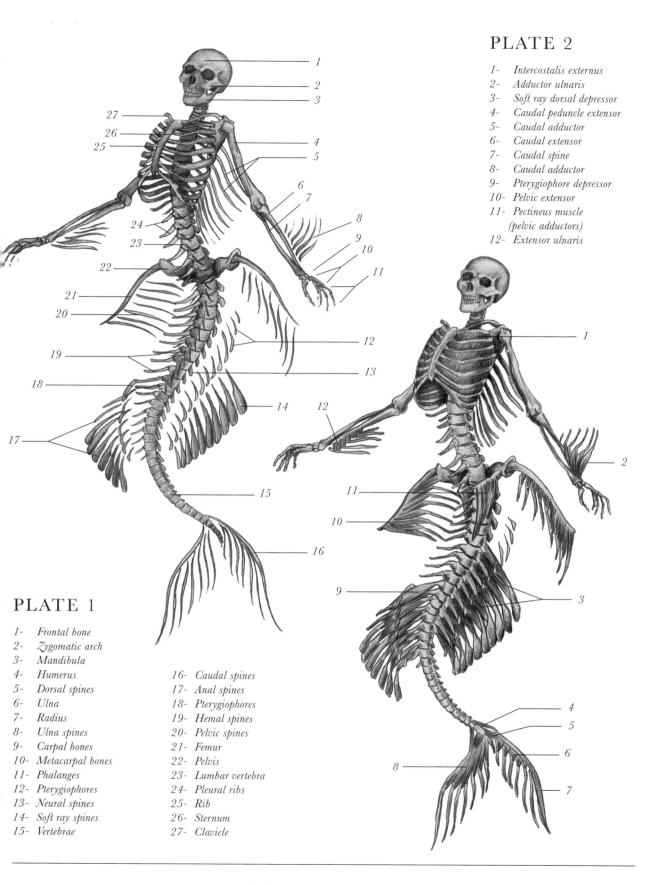

PLATE 2

1- *Intercostalis externus*
2- *Adductor ulnaris*
3- *Soft ray dorsal depressor*
4- *Caudal peduncle extensor*
5- *Caudal adductor*
6- *Caudal extensor*
7- *Caudal spine*
8- *Caudal adductor*
9- *Pterygiophore depressor*
10- *Pelvic extensor*
11- *Pectineus muscle*
    (pelvic adductors)
12- *Extensor ulnaris*

PLATE 1

1- *Frontal bone*
2- *Zygomatic arch*
3- *Mandibula*
4- *Humerus*
5- *Dorsal spines*
6- *Ulna*
7- *Radius*
8- *Ulna spines*
9- *Carpal bones*
10- *Metacarpal bones*
11- *Phalanges*
12- *Pterygiophores*
13- *Neural spines*
14- *Soft ray spines*
15- *Vertebrae*

16- *Caudal spines*
17- *Anal spines*
18- *Pterygiophores*
19- *Hemal spines*
20- *Pelvic spines*
21- *Femur*
22- *Pelvis*
23- *Lumbar vertebra*
24- *Pleural ribs*
25- *Rib*
26- *Sternum*
27- *Clavicle*

SIREN OCEANUS

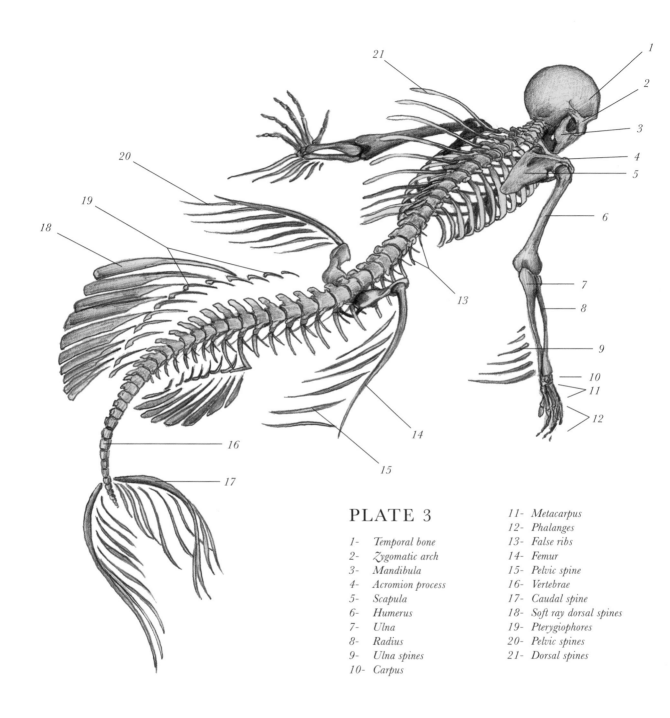

PLATE 3

1- Temporal bone
2- Zygomatic arch
3- Mandibula
4- Acromion process
5- Scapula
6- Humerus
7- Ulna
8- Radius
9- Ulna spines
10- Carpus

11- Metacarpus
12- Phalanges
13- False ribs
14- Femur
15- Pelvic spine
16- Vertebrae
17- Caudal spine
18- Soft ray dorsal spines
19- Pterygiophores
20- Pelvic spines
21- Dorsal spines

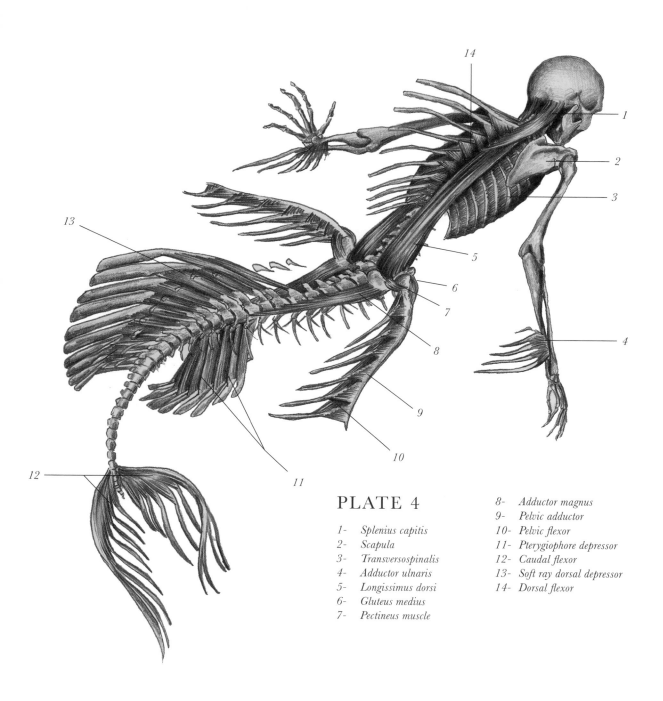

PLATE 4

1- *Splenius capitis*
2- *Scapula*
3- *Transversospinalis*
4- *Adductor ulnaris*
5- *Longissimus dorsi*
6- *Gluteus medius*
7- *Pectineus muscle*

8- *Adductor magnus*
9- *Pelvic adductor*
10- *Pelvic flexor*
11- *Pterygiophore depressor*
12- *Caudal flexor*
13- *Soft ray dorsal depressor*
14- *Dorsal flexor*

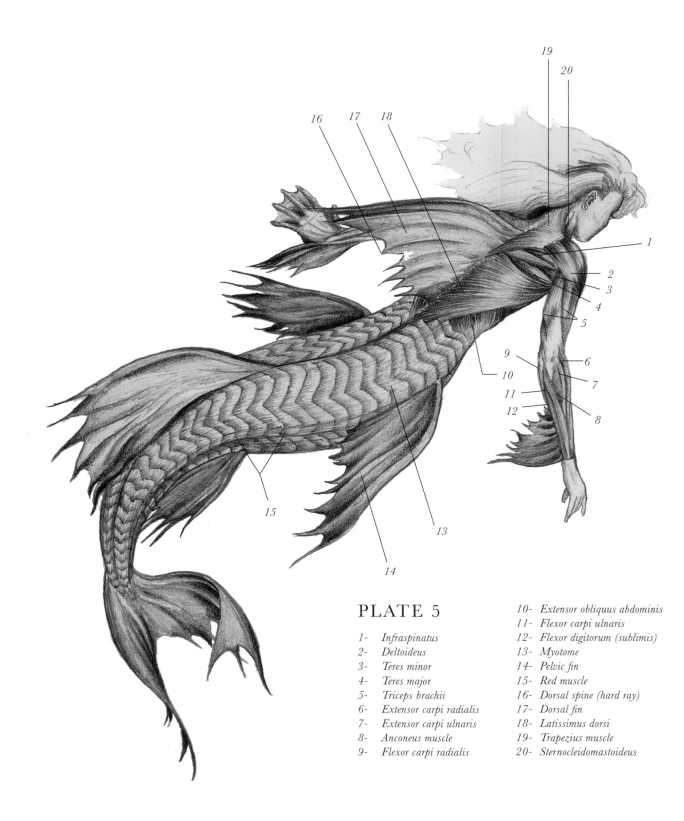

PLATE 5

1- *Infraspinatus*
2- *Deltoideus*
3- *Teres minor*
4- *Teres major*
5- *Triceps brachii*
6- *Extensor carpi radialis*
7- *Extensor carpi ulnaris*
8- *Anconeus muscle*
9- *Flexor carpi radialis*

10- *Extensor obliquus abdominis*
11- *Flexor carpi ulnaris*
12- *Flexor digitorum (sublimis)*
13- *Myotome*
14- *Pelvic fin*
15- *Red muscle*
16- *Dorsal spine (hard ray)*
17- *Dorsal fin*
18- *Latissimus dorsi*
19- *Trapezius muscle*
20- *Sternocleidomastoideus*

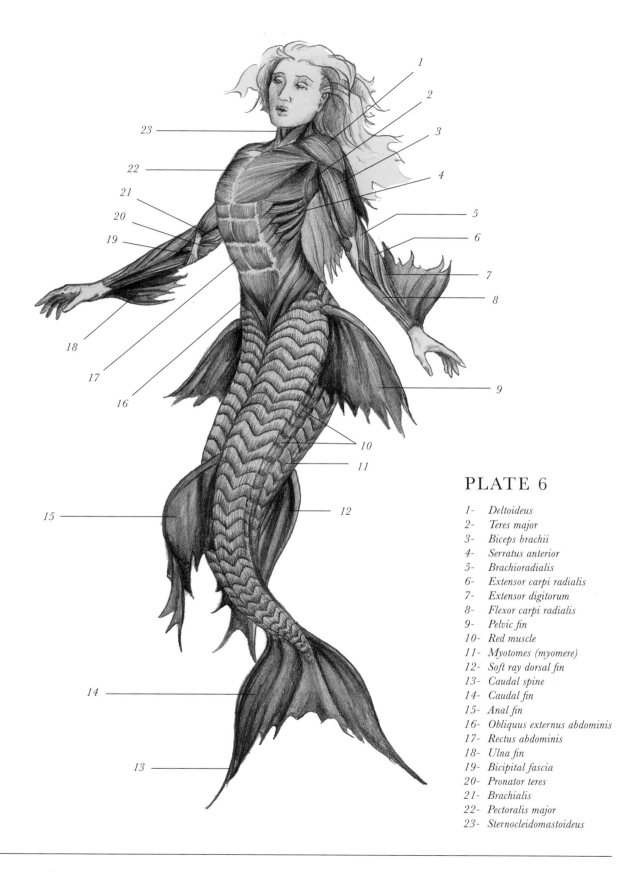

PLATE 6

1- *Deltoideus*
2- *Teres major*
3- *Biceps brachii*
4- *Serratus anterior*
5- *Brachioradialis*
6- *Extensor carpi radialis*
7- *Extensor digitorum*
8- *Flexor carpi radialis*
9- *Pelvic fin*
10- *Red muscle*
11- *Myotomes (myomere)*
12- *Soft ray dorsal fin*
13- *Caudal spine*
14- *Caudal fin*
15- *Anal fin*
16- *Obliquus externus abdominis*
17- *Rectus abdominis*
18- *Ulna fin*
19- *Bicipital fascia*
20- *Pronator teres*
21- *Brachialis*
22- *Pectoralis major*
23- *Sternocleidomastoideus*

SIREN OCEANUS

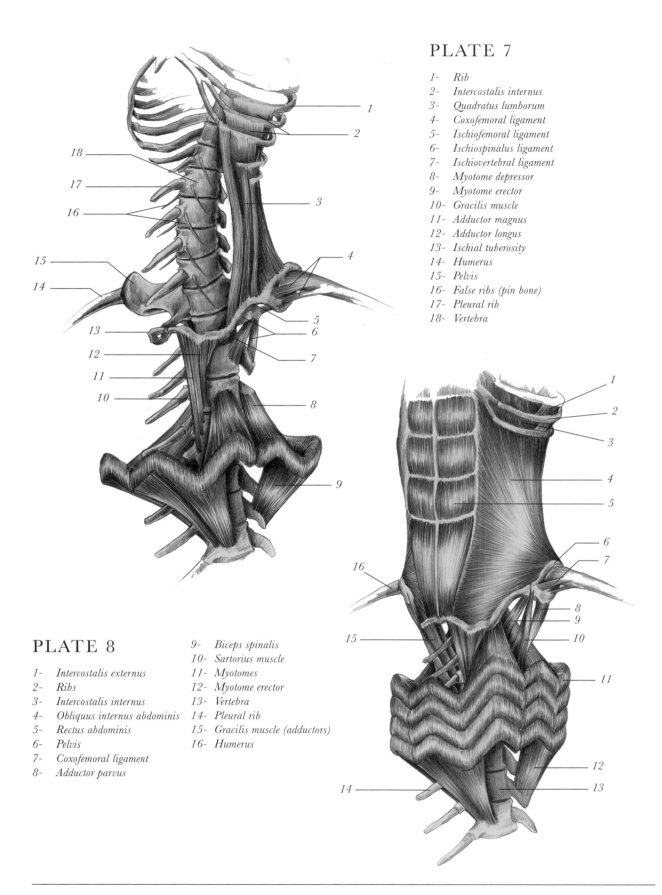

PLATE 7

1- Rib
2- Intercostalis internus
3- Quadratus lumborum
4- Coxofemoral ligament
5- Ischiofemoral ligament
6- Ischiospinalus ligament
7- Ischiovertebral ligament
8- Myotome depressor
9- Myotome erector
10- Gracilis muscle
11- Adductor magnus
12- Adductor longus
13- Ischial tuberosity
14- Humerus
15- Pelvis
16- False ribs (pin bone)
17- Pleural rib
18- Vertebra

PLATE 8

1- Intercostalis externus
2- Ribs
3- Intercostalis internus
4- Obliquus internus abdominis
5- Rectus abdominis
6- Pelvis
7- Coxofemoral ligament
8- Adductor parvus

9- Biceps spinalis
10- Sartorius muscle
11- Myotomes
12- Myotome erector
13- Vertebra
14- Pleural rib
15- Gracilis muscle (adductors)
16- Humerus

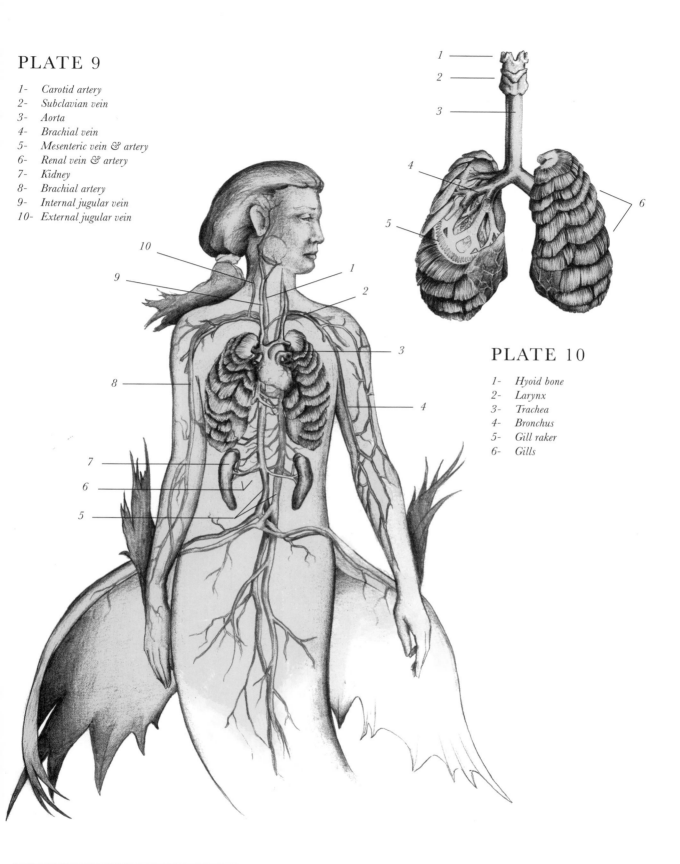

PLATE 9

1- *Carotid artery*
2- *Subclavian vein*
3- *Aorta*
4- *Brachial vein*
5- *Mesenteric vein & artery*
6- *Renal vein & artery*
7- *Kidney*
8- *Brachial artery*
9- *Internal jugular vein*
10- *External jugular vein*

PLATE 10

1- *Hyoid bone*
2- *Larynx*
3- *Trachea*
4- *Bronchus*
5- *Gill raker*
6- *Gills*

SIREN OCEANUS

PLATE 11

SIREN OCEANUS

PLATE 12

SIREN OCEANUS

Dr. Black's notes reference different kinds of satyrs and mention one that he claims to have found in Finland; however, there are no known remains of any specimen that Black may have studied. He refers to the satyr in a journal entry dated September 1906: "There are physiological aspects of this being that I, with my limited knowledge, could never quantify—only speculate. I suspect it held a heavenly song in its throat, a dancer's weight in its gait, and a child's mischief."

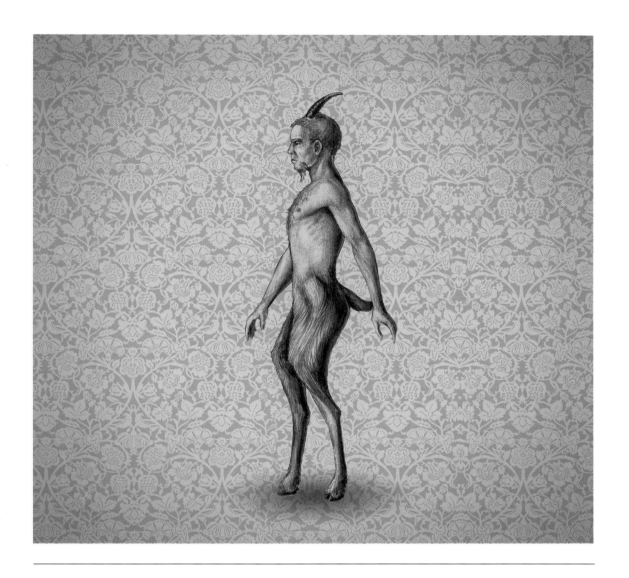

SATYRUS
HIRCINUS

KINGDOM	*Animalia*	**FAMILY**	*Faunus*
PHYLUM	*Vertebrata*	**GENUS**	*Satyrus*
CLASS	*Mammalia*	**SPECIES**	*Satyrus hircinus*
ORDER	*Artiodactyla*		

SHOWING MANY SIMILARITIES TO a minotaur, as a common goat does to a bull, the satyr's most important distinctions from the minotaur are its head and superior intelligence. I am well acquainted with the many interpretations of this creature; it has been portrayed in countless works of literature and stories for the stage. The species I studied (represented here) had the ears of a human, though goat-eared species are believed to exist. There may be other variations as well. I discovered a specimen resembling a ram near the border of Finland; there was too little remaining of the beast and, regrettably, it was not in a condition that permitted useful study or accurate representation. I have not yet come upon another like it.

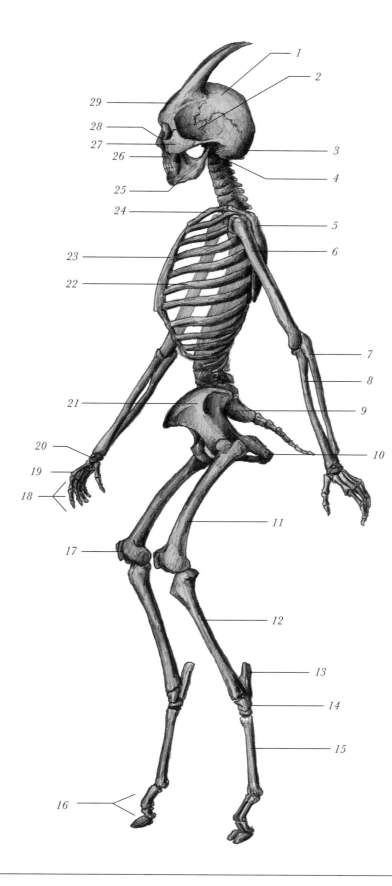

PLATE 1

1- *Parietal bone*
2- *Temporal bone*
3- *Occipital*
4- *Atlas*
5- *Scapula*
6- *Humerus*
7- *Ulna*
8- *Radius*
9- *Sacrum*
10- *Ischial tuber*
11- *Femur*
12- *Tibia*
13- *Calcaneus*
14- *Tarsal bones*
15- *Metatarsus*
16- *Phalanges*
17- *Patella*
18- *Phalanges*
19- *Metacarpal bones*
20- *Carpal bones*
21- *Pelvis*
22- *Ribs*
23- *Sternum*
24- *Clavicle*
25- *Mandibula*
26- *Maxilla*
27- *Zygomatic arch*
28- *Nasal*
29- *Frontal*

SATYRUS HIRCINUS

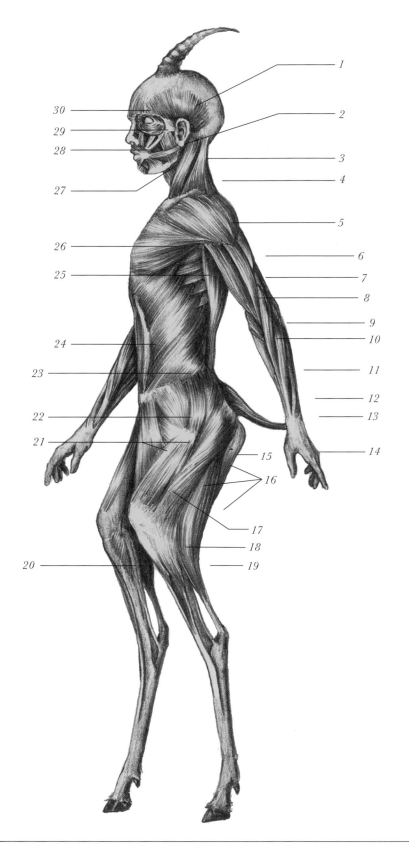

PLATE 2

1- *Temporalis*
2- *Masseter*
3- *Sternomastoid*
4- *Trapezius*
5- *Deltoideus*
6- *Triceps brachii*
7- *Brachialis*
8- *Biceps brachii*
9- *Brachioradialis*
10- *Pronator teres*
11- *Extensor carpi radialis longus*
12- *Extensor carpi radialis brevis*
13- *Adductor pollicis longus*
14- *Thenar*
15- *Semitendinosus*
16- *Biceps femoris*
17- *Quadriceps femoris*
18- *Peronaeus longus*
19- *Gastrocnemius*
20- *Popliteus*
21- *Tensor fasciae latae*
22- *Gluteus medius*
23- *Obliquus externus abdominis*
24- *Rectus abdominis*
25- *Serratus*
26- *Pectoralis*
27- *Triangularis*
28- *Orbicularis oris*
29- *Orbicularis oculi*
30- *Frontalis*

SATYRUS HIRCINUS

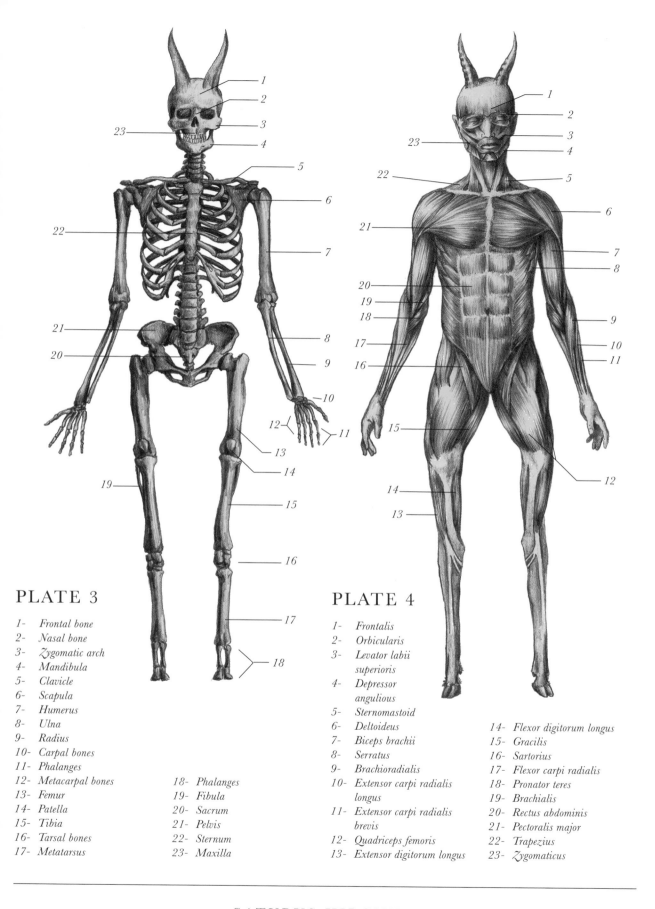

PLATE 3

1- Frontal bone
2- Nasal bone
3- Zygomatic arch
4- Mandibula
5- Clavicle
6- Scapula
7- Humerus
8- Ulna
9- Radius
10- Carpal bones
11- Phalanges
12- Metacarpal bones
13- Femur
14- Patella
15- Tibia
16- Tarsal bones
17- Metatarsus

18- Phalanges
19- Fibula
20- Sacrum
21- Pelvis
22- Sternum
23- Maxilla

PLATE 4

1- Frontalis
2- Orbicularis
3- Levator labii superioris
4- Depressor angulious
5- Sternomastoid
6- Deltoideus
7- Biceps brachii
8- Serratus
9- Brachioradialis
10- Extensor carpi radialis longus
11- Extensor carpi radialis brevis
12- Quadriceps femoris
13- Extensor digitorum longus

14- Flexor digitorum longus
15- Gracilis
16- Sartorius
17- Flexor carpi radialis
18- Pronator teres
19- Brachialis
20- Rectus abdominis
21- Pectoralis major
22- Trapezius
23- Zygomaticus

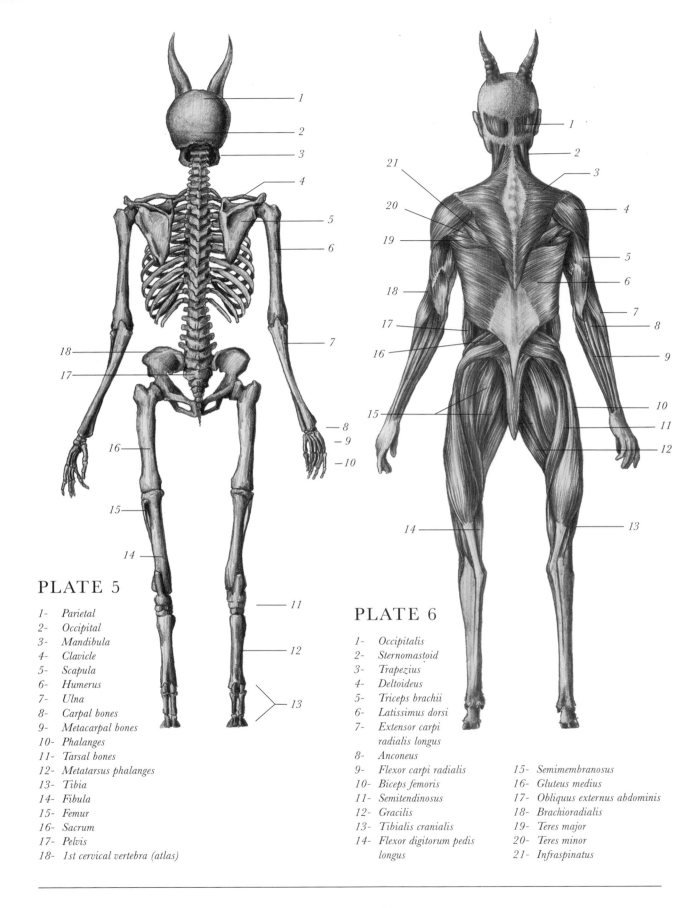

PLATE 5

1- *Parietal*
2- *Occipital*
3- *Mandibula*
4- *Clavicle*
5- *Scapula*
6- *Humerus*
7- *Ulna*
8- *Carpal bones*
9- *Metacarpal bones*
10- *Phalanges*
11- *Tarsal bones*
12- *Metatarsus phalanges*
13- *Tibia*
14- *Fibula*
15- *Femur*
16- *Sacrum*
17- *Pelvis*
18- *1st cervical vertebra (atlas)*

PLATE 6

1- *Occipitalis*
2- *Sternomastoid*
3- *Trapezius*
4- *Deltoideus*
5- *Triceps brachii*
6- *Latissimus dorsi*
7- *Extensor carpi radialis longus*
8- *Anconeus*
9- *Flexor carpi radialis*
10- *Biceps femoris*
11- *Semitendinosus*
12- *Gracilis*
13- *Tibialis cranialis*
14- *Flexor digitorum pedis longus*
15- *Semimembranosus*
16- *Gluteus medius*
17- *Obliquus externus abdominis*
18- *Brachioradialis*
19- *Teres major*
20- *Teres minor*
21- *Infraspinatus*

SATYRUS HIRCINUS

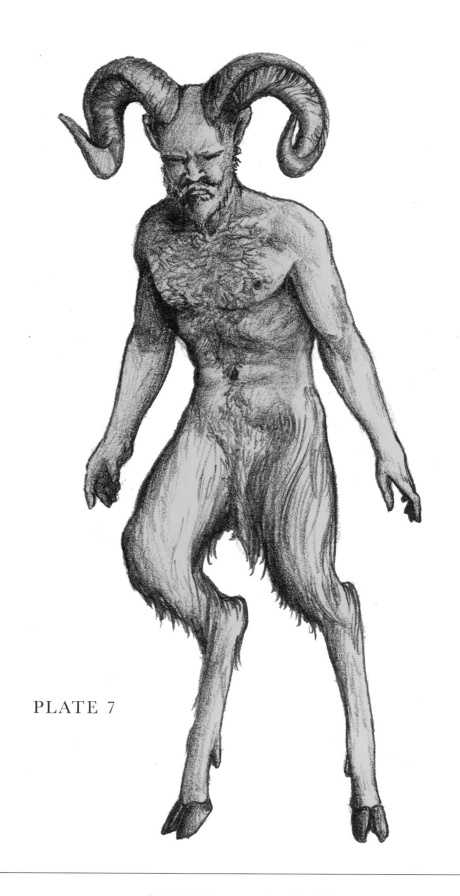

PLATE 7

SATYRUS HIRCINUS

BLACK'S MINOTAUR APPEARS TO BE A
TRAGIC BEAST INDEED. IT IS BESTOWED
WITH THE WORST TRAITS OF TWO
CREATURES, AND NONE OF THEIR GIFTS.
WHAT GOOD IS THE HUMAN BODY
WITHOUT THE HUMAN INTELLECT TO
COMMAND IT? WHAT GOOD IS THE MIND
OF A BULL WITHOUT THAT CREATURE'S
POWERFUL WEIGHT AND CHARGING
FORCE?

*There are additional shortcomings, as
well. The minotaur has no claws for
attacking or defense; it cannot fly or swim.
The existence of this beast seems difficult
to conceive.*

—SPENCER BLACK

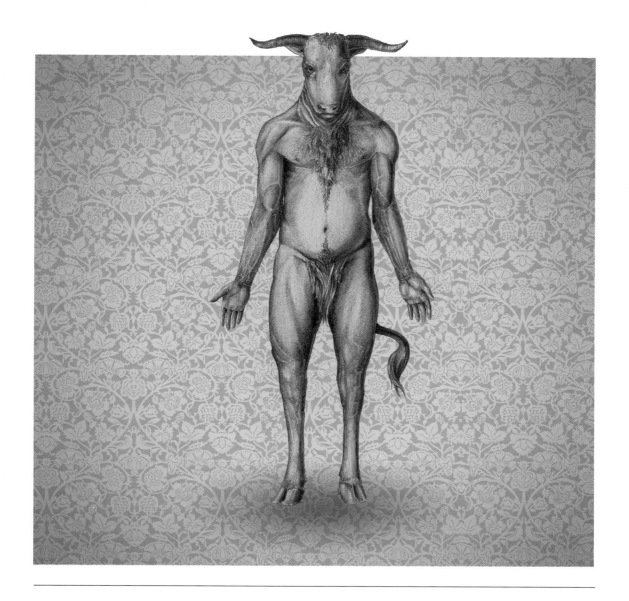

MINOTAURUS ASTERION

KINGDOM	*Animalia*	**FAMILY**	*Minos*
PHYLUM	*Vertebrata*	**GENUS**	*Minotaurus*
CLASS	*Mammalia*	**SPECIES**	*Minotaurus asterion*
ORDER	*Asterius*		

THIS SPECIMEN DEMONSTRATES the unique musculature necessary to support the minotaur's head in all of its possible functions, including combat. I have gathered incomplete segments of what appear to be creatures of the same species; thus far, I cannot conclude the existence of any variant to the species analyzed herein. The minotaur must have been unique despite conflicting accounts of its historical pedigree. It is important to consider the very real question of its ancestors, some of which may have possessed six limbs—four legs and two arms—as does the centaur. However, I have not yet come to know such a thing to be true.

Like many of the animals I have excavated or acquired from private collections, this specimen's preservation and condition have not allowed me to support a complete survey of the body. The soft tissues were so badly decomposed that I could ascertain nothing from the remains.

I would surmise that the ancient minotaur did not have a four-chambered stomach like its bovine cousin. I would consider it impractical to be a ruminant, having an upright disposition and two arms for the gathering and preparation of food. The minotaur was likely an omnivore; given its size, its disposition for predation may have been engendered by a scarcity of food. It is likely that it did not evolve balanced enough to adequately compete for food or defend itself: having only a simple brain and being bipedal, it would not have been able to run from an animal attack or devise a strategy or weapon to protect itself, as a beast with a greater propensity for intellect might have done.

MINOTAURUS ASTERION

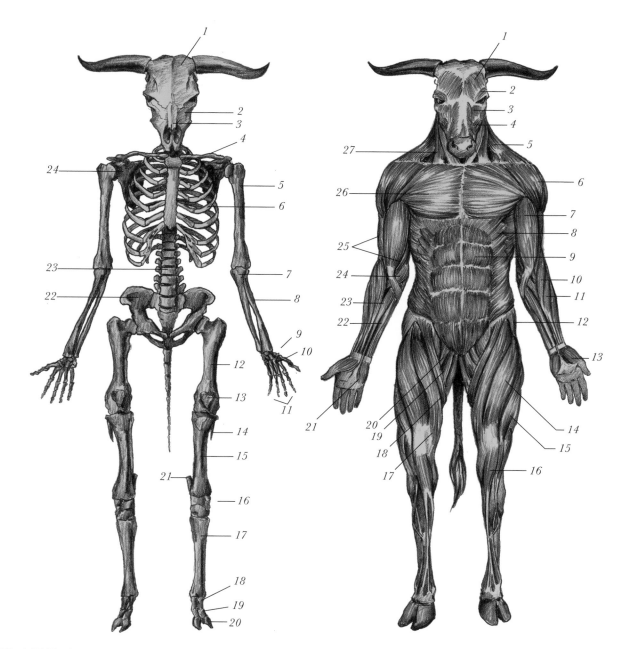

PLATE 1

1- *Frontal bone*
2- *Zygomatic arch*
3- *Nasal bone*
4- *Clavicle*
5- *Humerus*
6- *Ribs*
7- *Ulna*
8- *Radius*
9- *Carpal bones*
10- *Metacarpal bone*
11- *Phalanges*
12- *Femur*
13- *Patella*
14- *Fibula*
15- *Tibia*
16- *Tarsal bone*
17- *3rd & 4th metatarsal bones*
18- *1st phalanx*
19- *2nd phalanx*
20- *3rd phalanx*
21- *Olecranean tubor*
22- *Pelvis*
23- *Vertebrae*
24- *Scapula*

PLATE 2

1- *Frontalis*
2- *Orbicularis oculi*
3- *Zygomaticus major*
4- *Levator labii superioris*
5- *Trapezius*
6- *Deltoid*
7- *Biceps brachii*
8- *Serratus*
9- *Rectus abdominis*
10- *Brachioradialis*
11- *Extensor carpi radialis*
12- *Gluteus medius*
13- *Thenar*
14- *Rectus femoris*
15- *Vastus lateralis*
16- *Tibialis*
17- *Vastus medialis*
18- *Sartorius*
19- *Adductor longus*
20- *Pectineus*
21- *Hypothenar*
22- *Palmaris longus*
23- *Flexor carpi radialis*
24- *Pronator teres*
25- *Brachialis*
26- *Pectoralis major*
27- *Sternocleidomastoideus*

MINOTAURUS ASTERION

101

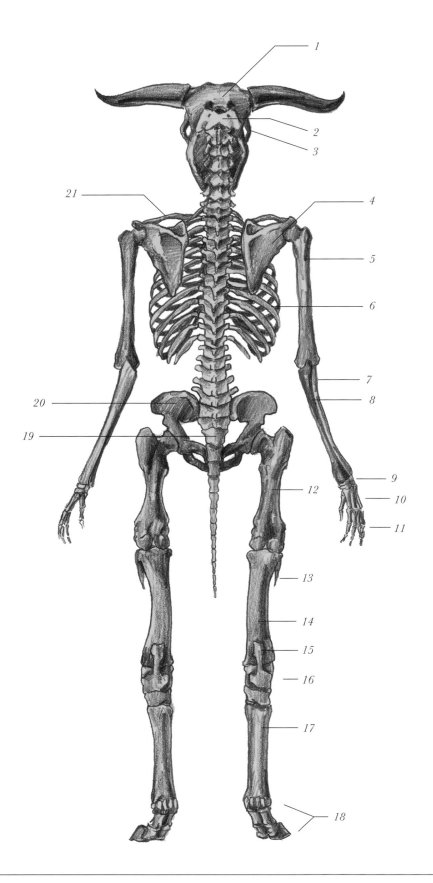

PLATE 3

1- *Parietale*
2- *1st cervical vertebra*
3- *Zygomatic bone*
4- *Scapula*
5- *Humerus*
6- *Rib*
7- *Radius*
8- *Ulna*
9- *Carpal bones*
10- *Metacarpal bones*
11- *Phalanges*
12- *Femur*
13- *Fibula*
14- *Tibia*
15- *Calcanean tubor*
16- *Tarsal bones*
17- *3rd & 4th metatarsal bones*
18- *Phalanges*
19- *Sacrum*
20- *Pelvis*
21- *Clavicle*

MINOTAURUS ASTERION

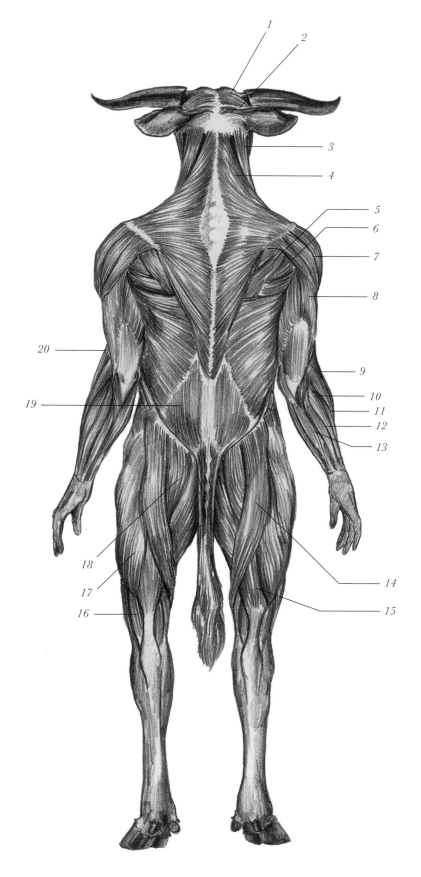

PLATE 4

1- *Obliquus capitis superior*
2- *Adductor of the auricle*
3- *Sternomastoid*
4- *Trapezius*
5- *Infraspinatus*
6- *Teres minor*
7- *Deltoid*
8- *Triceps brachii*
9- *Extensor carpi radialis longus*
10- *Extensor digitorum communis*
11- *Extensor carpi radialis brevis*
12- *Extensor carpi ulnaris*
13- *Flexor carpi ulnaris*
14- *Semitendinosus*
15- *Gastrocnemius*
16- *Tibialis cranialis*
17- *Biceps femoris*
18- *Semimembranosus*
19- *Sacrospinalis*
20- *Brachioradialis*

MINOTAURUS ASTERION

103

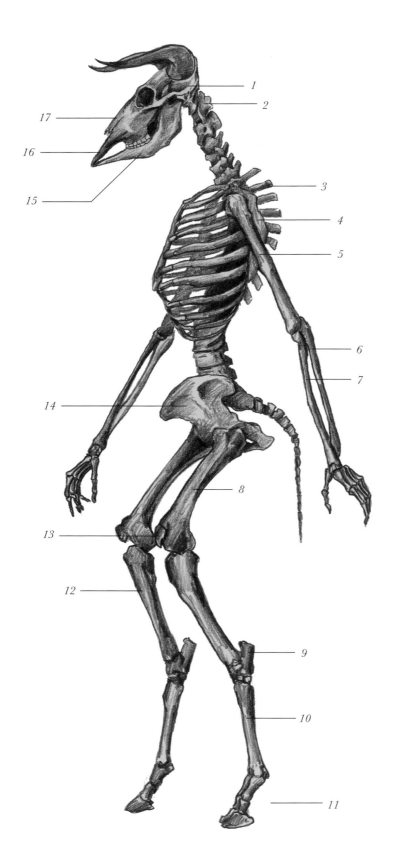

PLATE 5

1- Temporal bone
2- 1st cervical vertebra
3- 1st thoracic vertebra
4- Scapula
5- Humerus
6- Ulna
7- Radius
8- Femur
9- Calcanean tubor
10- 3rd & 4th metatarsal bone
11- Phalanges
12- Tibia
13- Patella
14- Pelvis
15- Incisor (lower jawbone)
16- Incisival bone
17- Nasal bone

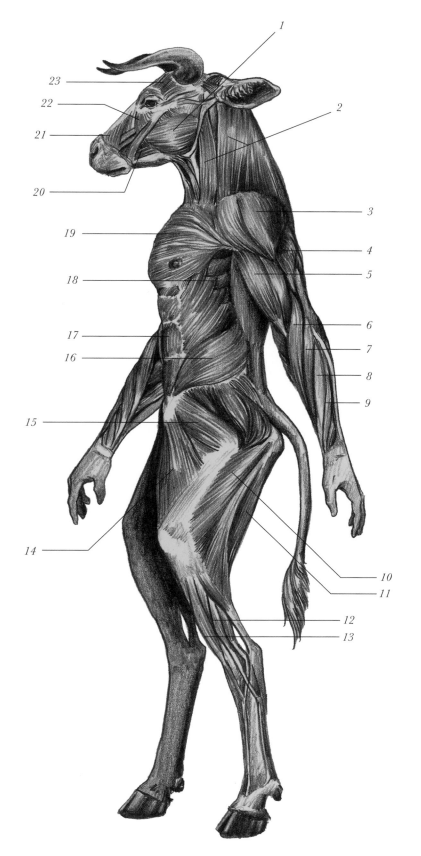

PLATE 6

1- *Masseter*
2- *Brachiocephalicus*
3- *Deltoid*
4- *Triceps brachii*
5- *Biceps brachii*
6- *Brachioradialis*
7- *Extensor carpi radialis longus*
8- *Extensor carpi radialis brevis*
9- *Adductor pollicis longus*
10- *Gluteobiceps*
11- *Semitendinosus*
12- *Peroneus longus*
13- *Peroneus tertius*
14- *Tensor fasciae latae*
15- *Gluteus medius*
16- *Obliquus externus abdominis*
17- *Rectus abdominis*
18- *Serratus*
19- *Pectoralis major*
20- *Buccinator*
21- *Levator nasolabialis*
22- *Zygomaticus minor*
23- *Frontalis*

MINOTAURUS ASTERION

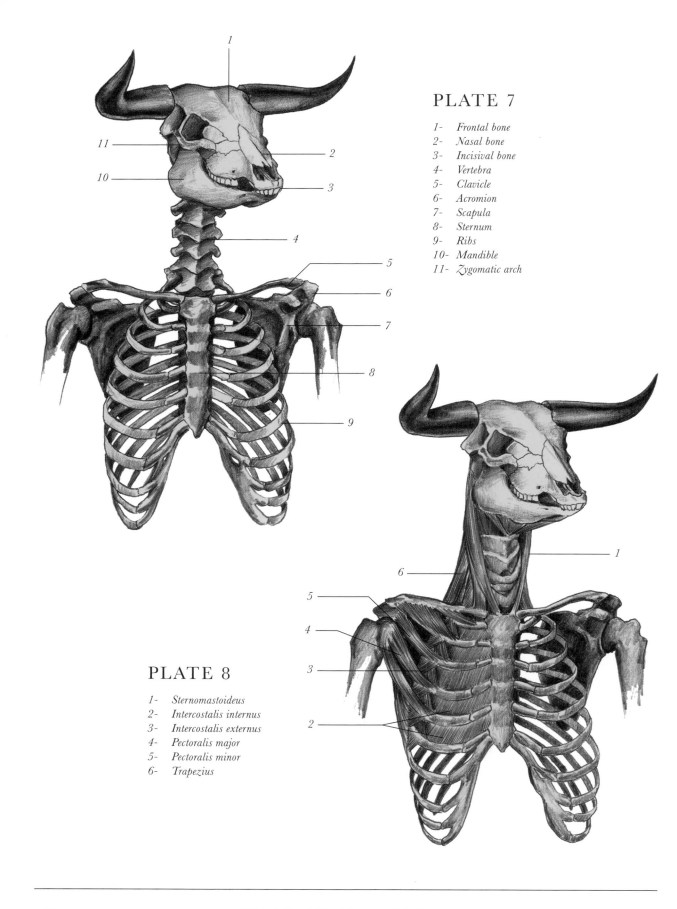

PLATE 7

1- *Frontal bone*
2- *Nasal bone*
3- *Incisival bone*
4- *Vertebra*
5- *Clavicle*
6- *Acromion*
7- *Scapula*
8- *Sternum*
9- *Ribs*
10- *Mandible*
11- *Zygomatic arch*

PLATE 8

1- *Sternomastoideus*
2- *Intercostalis internus*
3- *Intercostalis externus*
4- *Pectoralis major*
5- *Pectoralis minor*
6- *Trapezius*

MINOTAURUS ASTERION

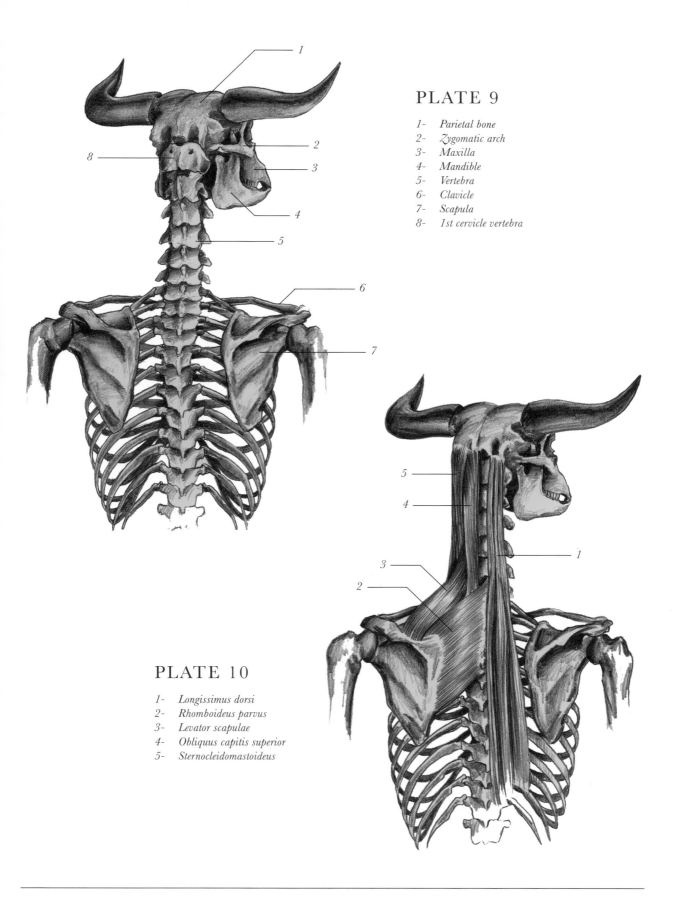

PLATE 9

1- Parietal bone
2- Zygomatic arch
3- Maxilla
4- Mandible
5- Vertebra
6- Clavicle
7- Scapula
8- 1st cervicle vertebra

PLATE 10

1- Longissimus dorsi
2- Rhomboideus parvus
3- Levator scapulae
4- Obliquus capitis superior
5- Sternocleidomastoideus

MINOTAURUS ASTERION

There are many interesting legends surrounding the origin of the Ganesha. In one story, the goddess Parvati created a boy from dust to guard her while she was bathing. Her husband, Shiva, came along and found a stranger waiting outside his wife's quarters; he attacked the boy, decapitating him. Upon learning the child was in fact Parvati's son, Shiva restored the boy, using the head of an elephant, and made him a leader.

The Ganesha was a drastic evolutionary juxtaposition of the natural physical form; man and elephant. Though Ganesha's origin is mere legend—it did not arise from the dust—truth is always hidden in the past.

—Spencer Black

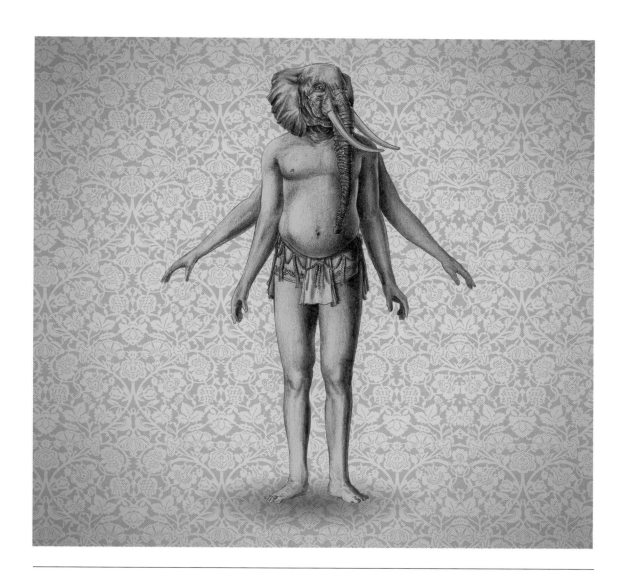

GANESHA ORIENTIS

KINGDOM	*Animalia*	**FAMILY**	*Homoeboreus*
PHYLUM	*Vertebrata*	**GENUS**	*Ganesha*
CLASS	*Mammalia*	**SPECIES**	*Ganesha orientis*
ORDER	*Proboscidea*		

MY STUDY OF THE ganesha answered one of my most persistent questions regarding the bone matter in a host of creatures: How can such small and slight bones support such massive appendages and disproportionately sized heads? It seems the ganesha had a sinewy fiber woven throughout its bone structure, independent of the ligament and tendon systems. This sinew acted as a resistance barrier for undue or excessive strain—much as a splint protects a broken limb. The sinew functioned not unlike an external skeletal structure for the bone; this material helps explain how many animals could withstand excess strain and torsion. Unfortunately, I do not know of any living creature that evolved with this material.

My specimen is one of the great treasures of the east. Though only a portion of the creature was recovered, it was well-preserved, and wrapped in hundreds of yards of decayed cloth. Future discoveries are a possibility. I happened upon chance to come to the tomb of one, and surely there are many more.

The ganesha's skull would not have housed what would be classified as either a human or an elephant brain; however, the shape and position of the brain, especially the cerebral cortex, is cause for more extensive study and additional research. I can conclude that the animal was more than likely of a high intellect, confounding one who considers why it failed to prosper as a species.

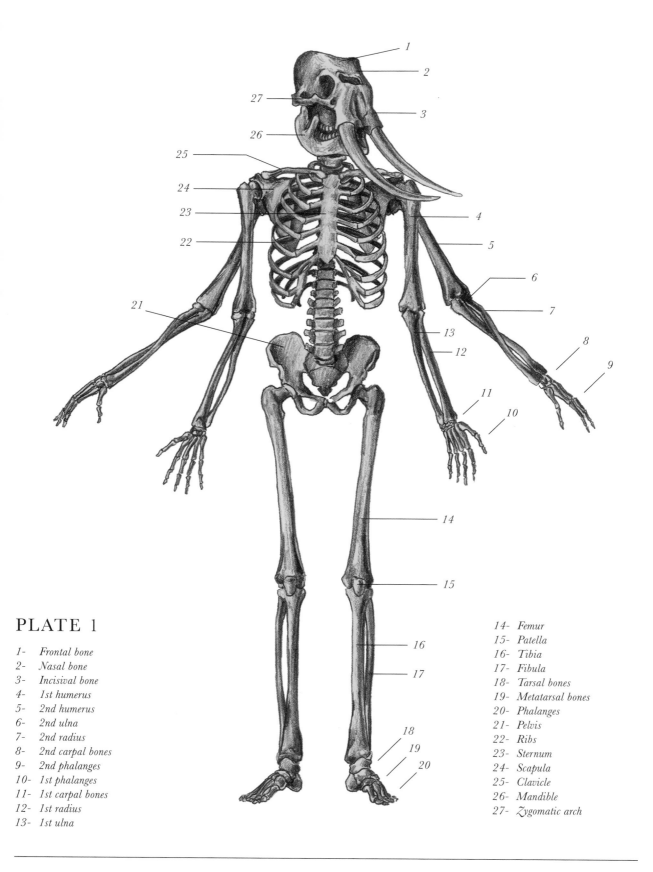

PLATE 1

1- Frontal bone
2- Nasal bone
3- Incisival bone
4- 1st humerus
5- 2nd humerus
6- 2nd ulna
7- 2nd radius
8- 2nd carpal bones
9- 2nd phalanges
10- 1st phalanges
11- 1st carpal bones
12- 1st radius
13- 1st ulna

14- Femur
15- Patella
16- Tibia
17- Fibula
18- Tarsal bones
19- Metatarsal bones
20- Phalanges
21- Pelvis
22- Ribs
23- Sternum
24- Scapula
25- Clavicle
26- Mandible
27- Zygomatic arch

GANESHA ORIENTIS

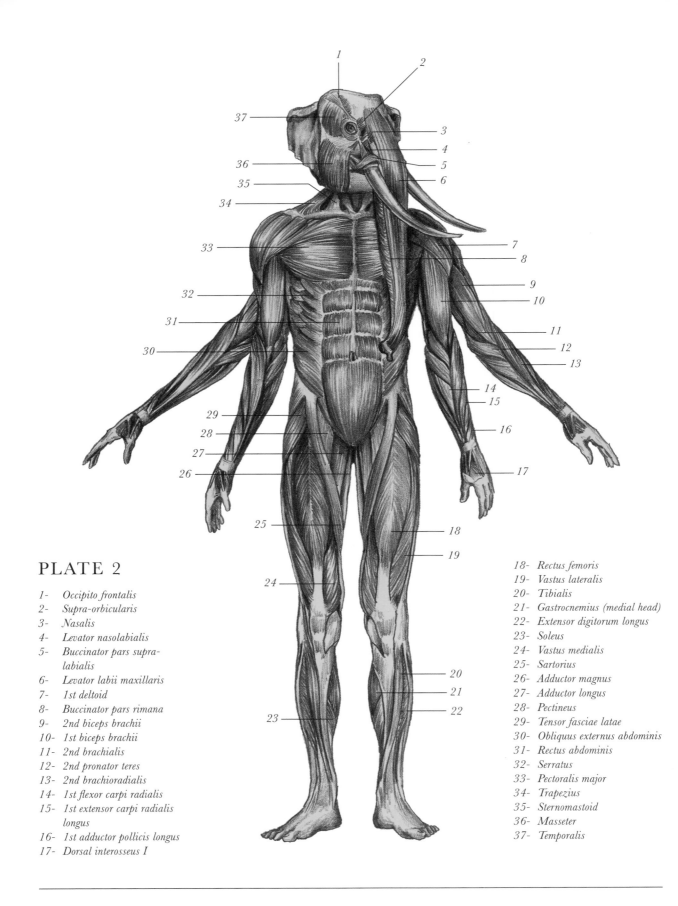

PLATE 2

1- Occipito frontalis
2- Supra-orbicularis
3- Nasalis
4- Levator nasolabialis
5- Buccinator pars supra-
   labialis
6- Levator labii maxillaris
7- 1st deltoid
8- Buccinator pars rimana
9- 2nd biceps brachii
10- 1st biceps brachii
11- 2nd brachialis
12- 2nd pronator teres
13- 2nd brachioradialis
14- 1st flexor carpi radialis
15- 1st extensor carpi radialis
    longus
16- 1st adductor pollicis longus
17- Dorsal interosseus I

18- Rectus femoris
19- Vastus lateralis
20- Tibialis
21- Gastrocnemius (medial head)
22- Extensor digitorum longus
23- Soleus
24- Vastus medialis
25- Sartorius
26- Adductor magnus
27- Adductor longus
28- Pectineus
29- Tensor fasciae latae
30- Obliquus externus abdominis
31- Rectus abdominis
32- Serratus
33- Pectoralis major
34- Trapezius
35- Sternomastoid
36- Masseter
37- Temporalis

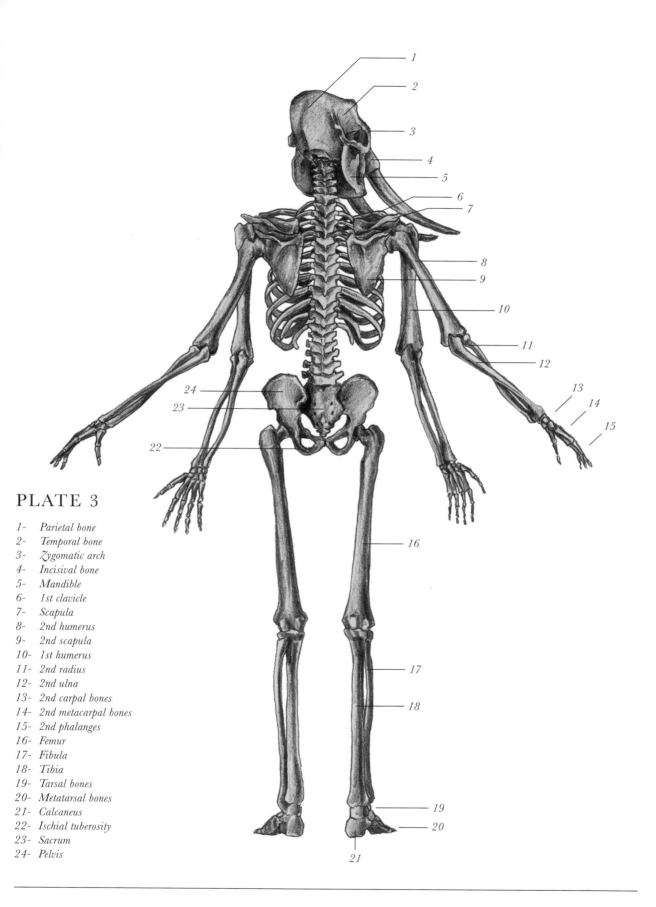

PLATE 3

1- Parietal bone
2- Temporal bone
3- Zygomatic arch
4- Incisival bone
5- Mandible
6- 1st clavicle
7- Scapula
8- 2nd humerus
9- 2nd scapula
10- 1st humerus
11- 2nd radius
12- 2nd ulna
13- 2nd carpal bones
14- 2nd metacarpal bones
15- 2nd phalanges
16- Femur
17- Fibula
18- Tibia
19- Tarsal bones
20- Metatarsal bones
21- Calcaneus
22- Ischial tuberosity
23- Sacrum
24- Pelvis

GANESHA ORIENTIS

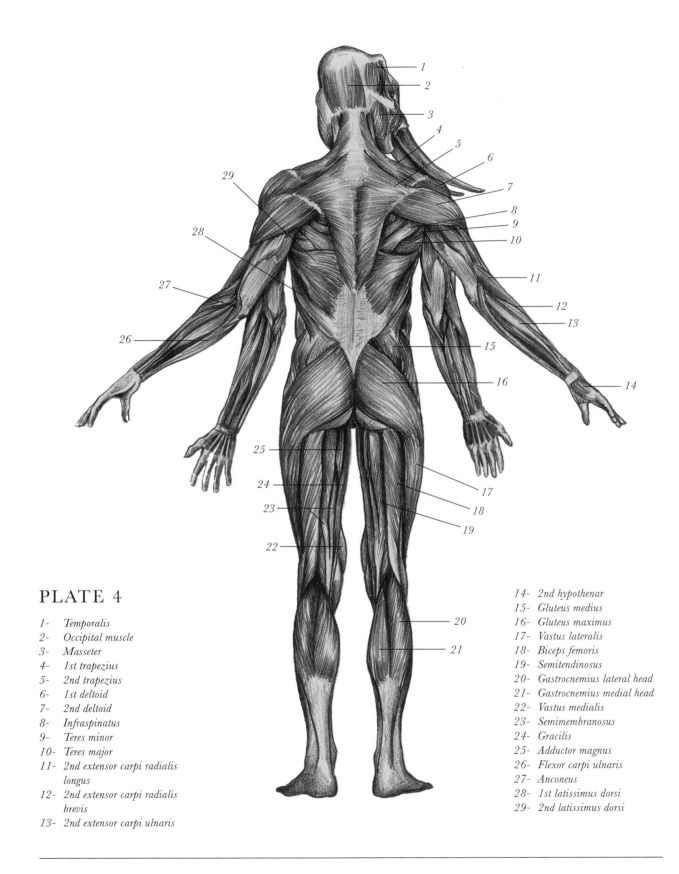

PLATE 4

1- Temporalis
2- Occipital muscle
3- Masseter
4- 1st trapezius
5- 2nd trapezius
6- 1st deltoid
7- 2nd deltoid
8- Infraspinatus
9- Teres minor
10- Teres major
11- 2nd extensor carpi radialis
    longus
12- 2nd extensor carpi radialis
    brevis
13- 2nd extensor carpi ulnaris

14- 2nd hypothenar
15- Gluteus medius
16- Gluteus maximus
17- Vastus lateralis
18- Biceps femoris
19- Semitendinosus
20- Gastrocnemius lateral head
21- Gastrocnemius medial head
22- Vastus medialis
23- Semimembranosus
24- Gracilis
25- Adductor magnus
26- Flexor carpi ulnaris
27- Anconeus
28- 1st latissimus dorsi
29- 2nd latissimus dorsi

GANESHA ORIENTIS

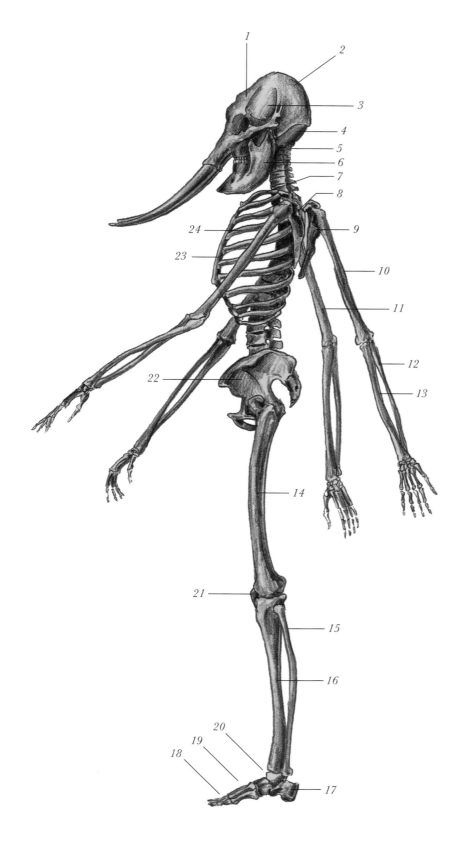

PLATE 5

1- Frontal bone
2- Parietal bone
3- Temporal bone
4- Occipital bone
5- Axis
6- Mandible
7- 1st clavicle
8- 1st scapula
9- 2nd scapula
10- 2nd humerus
11- 1st humerus
12- 2nd radius
13- 2nd ulna
14- Femur
15- Fibula
16- Tibia
17- Calcaneus
18- Phalanges
19- Metatarsals
20- Carpal bones
21- Patella
22- Pelvis
23- Sternum
24- Ribs

GANESHA ORIENTIS

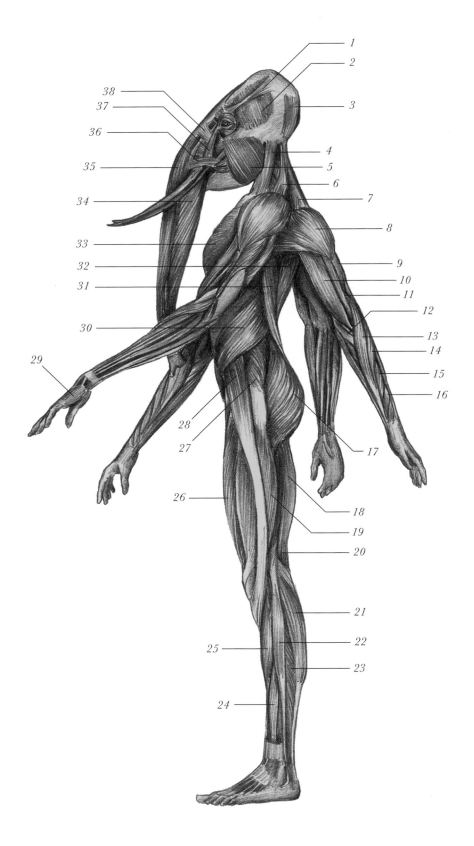

PLATE 6

1- *Occipitofrontalis*
2- *Temporalis*
3- *Occipitalis*
4- *Sternomastoid*
5- *Masseter*
6- *1st trapezius*
7- *2nd trapezius*
8- *2nd deltoid*
9- *2nd triceps brachii*
10- *2nd biceps brachii*
11- *2nd brachialis*
12- *2nd pronator teres*
13- *2nd brachioradialis*
14- *2nd extensor carpi radialis longus*
15- *2nd extensor carpi radialis brevis*
16- *Adductor pollicis longus*
17- *Gluteus maximus*
18- *Biceps femoris*
19- *Vastus lateralis*
20- *Semimembranosus*
21- *Gastrocnemius*
22- *Peroneus longus*
23- *Soleus*
24- *Extensor digitorum longus*
25- *Tibialis*
26- *Rectus femoris*
27- *Gluteus medius*
28- *Tensor fasiae latae*
29- *Hypthenar*
30- *Obliquus externus abdominis*
31- *1st latissimus dorsi*
32- *2nd latissimus dorsi*
33- *Pectoralis major*
34- *Buccinator, pars rimana*
35- *Levator labii maxillaris*
36- *Buccinator, pars supra-labialis*
37- *Levator nasolabialis*
38- *Nasalis*

GANESHA ORIENTIS

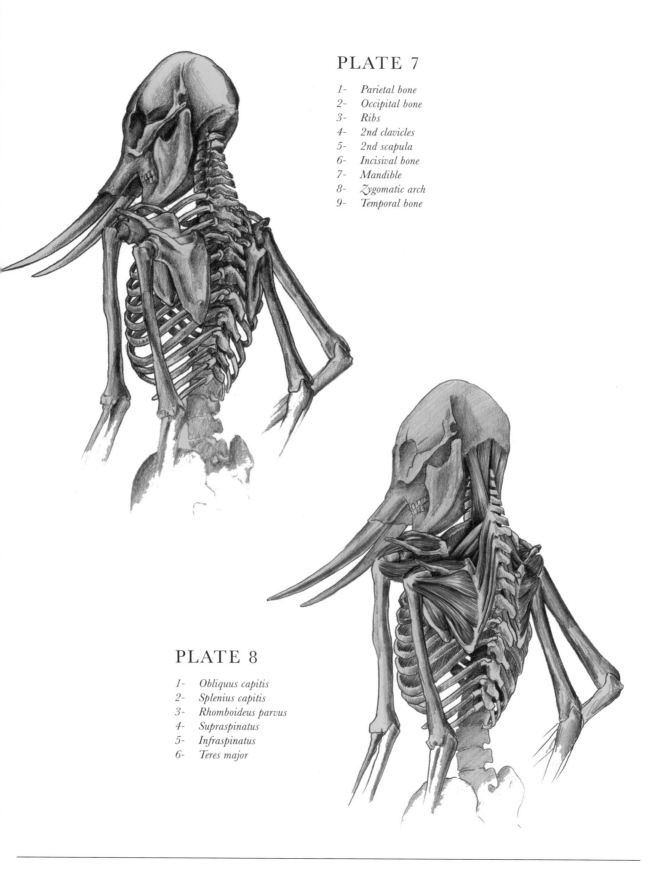

PLATE 7

1- *Parietal bone*
2- *Occipital bone*
3- *Ribs*
4- *2nd clavicles*
5- *2nd scapula*
6- *Incisival bone*
7- *Mandible*
8- *Zygomatic arch*
9- *Temporal bone*

PLATE 8

1- *Obliquus capitis*
2- *Splenius capitis*
3- *Rhomboideus parvus*
4- *Supraspinatus*
5- *Infraspinatus*
6- *Teres major*

GANESHA ORIENTIS

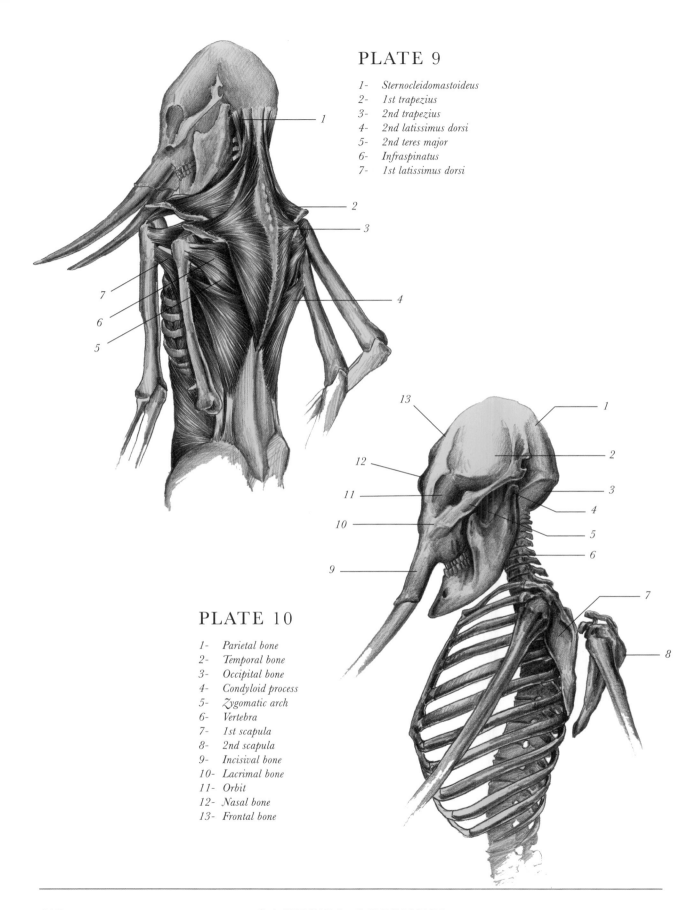

PLATE 9

1- *Sternocleidomastoideus*
2- *1st trapezius*
3- *2nd trapezius*
4- *2nd latissimus dorsi*
5- *2nd teres major*
6- *Infraspinatus*
7- *1st latissimus dorsi*

PLATE 10

1- *Parietal bone*
2- *Temporal bone*
3- *Occipital bone*
4- *Condyloid process*
5- *Zygomatic arch*
6- *Vertebra*
7- *1st scapula*
8- *2nd scapula*
9- *Incisival bone*
10- *Lacrimal bone*
11- *Orbit*
12- *Nasal bone*
13- *Frontal bone*

PLATE 11

1- *Temporalis*
2- *Masseter*
3- *Scalenus medius*
4- *Scalenus anterior*
5- *2nd pectoralis major*
6- *Infraspinatus*
7- *Biceps brachii*
8- *1st latissimus dorsi*
9- *2nd latissimus dorsi*
10- *Quadratus lumborum*
11- *Obliquus internus abdominis*
12- *Intercostalis internus*

13- *Triceps brachii*
14- *2nd pectoralis major*
15- *Buccinator, pars rimana*
16- *1st pectoralis major*
17- *Buccinator, pars supra-labialis*
18- *Levator labii maxillaris*
19- *Frontalis muscle*

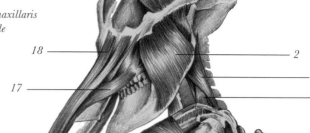

PLATE 12

1- *Pectoralis major*
2- *Infraspinatus*
3- *Teres major*
4- *Brachialis*
5- *Triceps brachii*
6- *Pectoralis minor*

GANESHA ORIENTIS

TODAY THERE ARE NO KNOWN SPECIES WITH
MULTIPLE HEADS, ALTHOUGH TWO- OR
THREE-HEADED MUTATIONS OF EXISTING
CREATURES ARE NOT UNCOMMON (THIS
CONDITION IS KNOWN AS "POLYCEPHALY").
OFTEN THE MUTATIONS ARE BORN WITH
THEIR HEADS FUSED TOGETHER. SADLY,
THESE MUTATIONS RARELY LIVE FOR VERY
LONG.

IN THE NEXT TWO CHAPTERS, DR.
BLACK EXPLORES A PAIR OF THREE-
HEADED CREATURES—THE CHIMÆRA
AND THE CERBERUS. HE WAS ADAMANT
THAT THESE SPECIES WERE NOT RANDOM
MUTATIONS BUT RATHER FULLY FORMED
ANIMALS.

CHIMÆRA
INCENDIARIUS

KINGDOM	Animalia	FAMILY	Incendium
PHYLUM	Vertebrata	GENUS	Chimæra
CLASS	Echidnæ	SPECIES	Chimæra incendiarius
ORDER	Praesidium		

WHAT CHALLENGE LIES before whoever ponders this beast! Why would nature require it to be shaped in such a fashion? Its form is confounding and distasteful. Nonetheless, all mysteries ought to be solved; their secrets should be revealed.

Without having the great privilege and scientific benefit of studying the creature whilst it was alive and moving before me, I am unable to understand how it managed the apparent dilemma of three brains, three wills, and only one body to command. This is a great point of intrigue to me, and a burden on my ever-increasingly curious studies.

I find it baffling that the tail of the creature has the structure of that belonging to a serpent, and yet the chimæra has none of a serpent's functionality; it could neither slither nor coil upon the ground. I suspect that the tail is merely a system used for balance.

The musculature of the lion's head seems to outweigh (by measure of weight, proportion, and tension) the other two heads. I concluded that the central vertebral joint, the *trithoracic vertebra*, can resist enough torsion to accommodate the animal moderately but not effectively.

The diet is another curiosity. All three heads, whose origins are from creatures of differing diets, must surely share a common digestive tract and other similar requirements for basic functionality. I imagine there must have been ample opportunity to benefit from such an arrangement; the goat could graze whilst the lion rested, perhaps.

It is likely that a more modest, necessary, and adaptable animal evolved from the chimæra, though I have no evidence to that end. It is my belief that the chimæra could not have survived a respectable length of time in its environment.

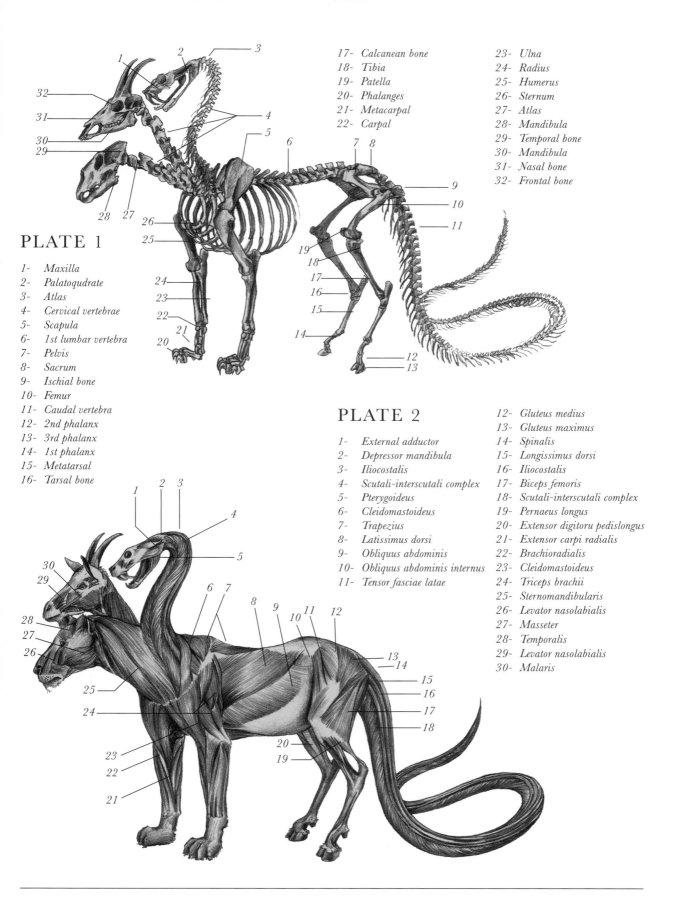

17- Calcanean bone
18- Tibia
19- Patella
20- Phalanges
21- Metacarpal
22- Carpal

23- Ulna
24- Radius
25- Humerus
26- Sternum
27- Atlas
28- Mandibula
29- Temporal bone
30- Mandibula
31- Nasal bone
32- Frontal bone

PLATE 1

1- Maxilla
2- Palatoqudrate
3- Atlas
4- Cervical vertebrae
5- Scapula
6- 1st lumbar vertebra
7- Pelvis
8- Sacrum
9- Ischial bone
10- Femur
11- Caudal vertebra
12- 2nd phalanx
13- 3rd phalanx
14- 1st phalanx
15- Metatarsal
16- Tarsal bone

PLATE 2

1- External adductor
2- Depressor mandibula
3- Iliocostalis
4- Scutali-interscutali complex
5- Pterygoideus
6- Cleidomastoideus
7- Trapezius
8- Latissimus dorsi
9- Obliquus abdominis
10- Obliquus abdominis internus
11- Tensor fasciae latae

12- Gluteus medius
13- Gluteus maximus
14- Spinalis
15- Longissimus dorsi
16- Iliocostalis
17- Biceps femoris
18- Scutali-interscutali complex
19- Pernaeus longus
20- Extensor digitoru pedislongus
21- Extensor carpi radialis
22- Brachioradialis
23- Cleidomastoideus
24- Triceps brachii
25- Sternomandibularis
26- Levator nasolabialis
27- Masseter
28- Temporalis
29- Levator nasolabialis
30- Malaris

CHIMÆRA INCENDIARIUS

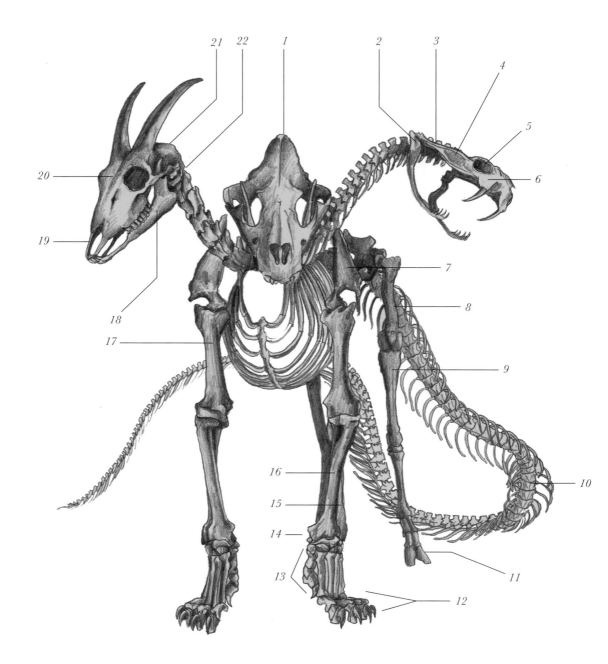

PLATE 3

1- Occipital bone
2- Mandibula
3- Pterygoid
4- Transpalatine
5- Prefrontal
6- Maxilla

7- Scapula
8- Femur
9- Tibia
10- Caudal vertebra
11- Distal phalanx
12- Phalanges
13- Metacarpal bones
14- Carpal bones

15- Ulna
16- Radius
17- Humerus
18- Mandibula
19- Incisive bone
20- Frontal bone
21- Occipital bone
22- Atlas

CHIMÆRA INCENDIARIUS

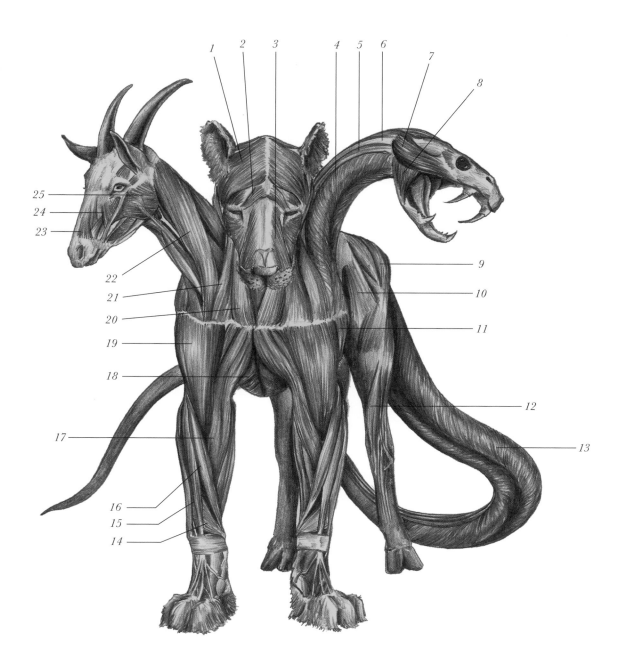

PLATE 4

1- Temporalis
2- Corrugator supercilii
3- Levator nasolabialis
4- Scutali-interscutali complex
5- Iliocostalis
6- Longissimus dorsi

7- External adductor
8- Pterygoideus
9- Biceps femoris
10- Tensor fasciae latae
11- Deltoideus
12- Extensor digitorum pedislongus
13- Scutali-interscutali complex

14- Adductor pollicis longus
15- Extensor digitorum communis
16- Brachioradialis
17- Pronator teres
18- Pectoralis major
19- Cleidomastoideus
20- Sternomandibularis

21- Cleidomastoideus
22- Brachiocephalicus
23- Levator nasolabialis
24- Malaris
25- Masseter

CHIMÆRA INCENDIARIUS

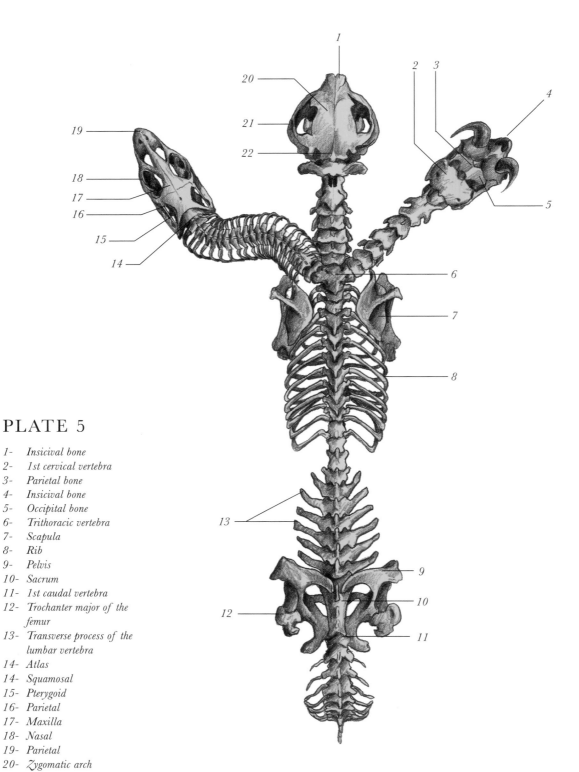

PLATE 5

1- *Insicival bone*
2- *1st cervical vertebra*
3- *Parietal bone*
4- *Insicival bone*
5- *Occipital bone*
6- *Trithoracic vertebra*
7- *Scapula*
8- *Rib*
9- *Pelvis*
10- *Sacrum*
11- *1st caudal vertebra*
12- *Trochanter major of the*
    femur
13- *Transverse process of the*
    lumbar vertebra
14- *Atlas*
14- *Squamosal*
15- *Pterygoid*
16- *Parietal*
17- *Maxilla*
18- *Nasal*
19- *Parietal*
20- *Zygomatic arch*
21- *Occipital*
22- *Atlas (1st cervical vertebra)*

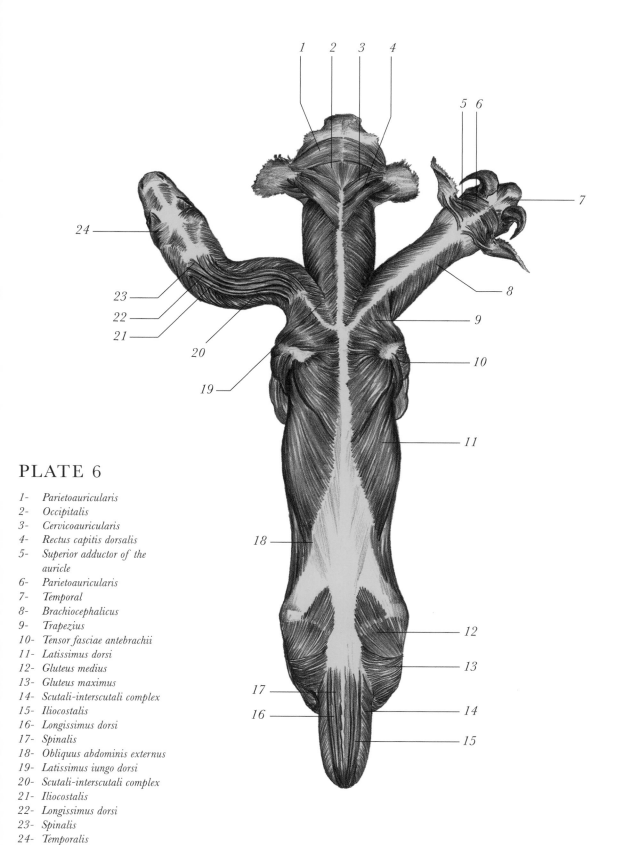

PLATE 6

1- *Parietoauricularis*
2- *Occipitalis*
3- *Cervicoauricularis*
4- *Rectus capitis dorsalis*
5- *Superior adductor of the auricle*
6- *Parietoauricularis*
7- *Temporal*
8- *Brachiocephalicus*
9- *Trapezius*
10- *Tensor fasciae antebrachii*
11- *Latissimus dorsi*
12- *Gluteus medius*
13- *Gluteus maximus*
14- *Scutali-interscutali complex*
15- *Iliocostalis*
16- *Longissimus dorsi*
17- *Spinalis*
18- *Obliquus abdominis externus*
19- *Latissimus iungo dorsi*
20- *Scutali-interscutali complex*
21- *Iliocostalis*
22- *Longissimus dorsi*
23- *Spinalis*
24- *Temporalis*

CHIMÆRA INCENDIARIUS

127

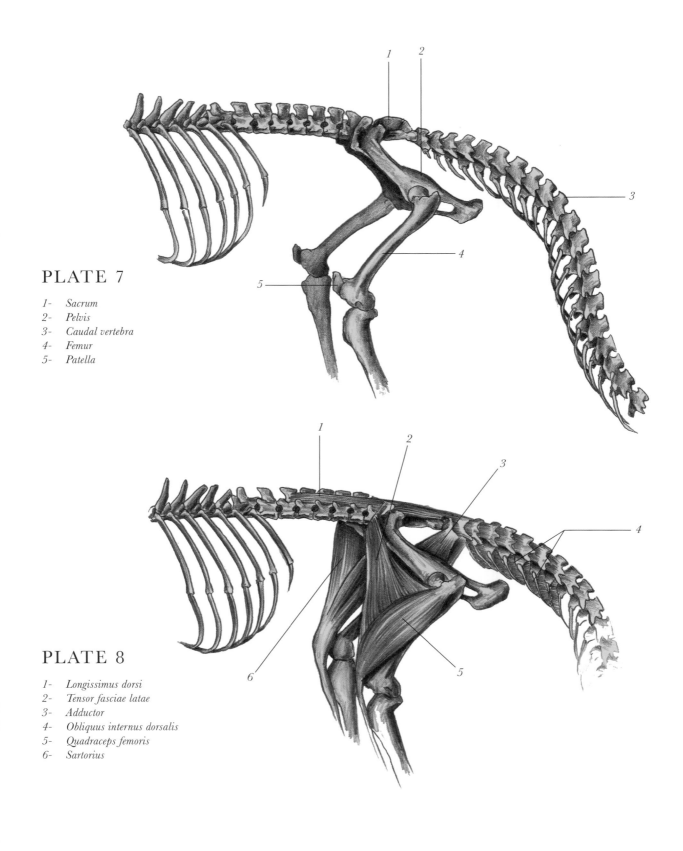

PLATE 7

1- *Sacrum*
2- *Pelvis*
3- *Caudal vertebra*
4- *Femur*
5- *Patella*

PLATE 8

1- *Longissimus dorsi*
2- *Tensor fasciae latae*
3- *Adductor*
4- *Obliquus internus dorsalis*
5- *Quadraceps femoris*
6- *Sartorius*

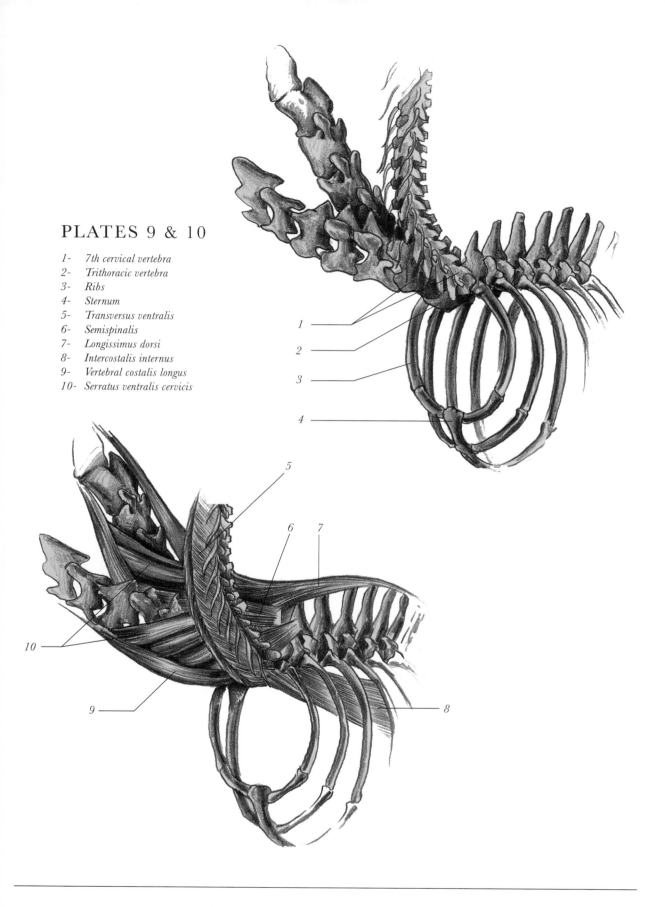

PLATES 9 & 10

1- *7th cervical vertebra*
2- *Trithoracic vertebra*
3- *Ribs*
4- *Sternum*
5- *Transversus ventralis*
6- *Semispinalis*
7- *Longissimus dorsi*
8- *Intercostalis internus*
9- *Vertebral costalis longus*
10- *Serratus ventralis cervicis*

CHIMÆRA INCENDIARIUS

Like the chimæra, the creature known as the cerberus also has three heads—only in this case, the heads all belong to the same species. Black experimented with dogs on several occasions. We know of the work done with Darwin's Beagle, but we do not know the full extent of Black's experimentation with polycephalous creatures.

CANIS
HADES

KINGDOM	*Animalia*	**FAMILY**	*Canidæ*
PHYLUM	*Vertebrata*	**GENUS**	*Canis*
CLASS	*Echidnæ*	**SPECIES**	*Canis hades*
ORDER	*Praesidium*		

I ORIGINALLY BELIEVED THE hell-hound was a singular creation, much like the ganesha and the chimæra. However, I had the peculiar fortune to come into the possession of eight beasts, all of which appeared to have perished together as a pack. Several of the beasts had two or three heads, and one of the dogs possessed six. A specimen with three heads and a serpent tail is the case for study here.

There must be some element in the bone, blood, or brain of the cerberus and the chimæra that allowed for the growth of multiple heads. These creatures are not mere mutations born of unnatural conditions; their design is far too deliberate and intentional. Despite their superficial similarities I have no evidence that these two creatures are closely related. I am not related to a fish simply because we both have a single head.

The cerberus would have been warm blooded with many traits likened to other mammals: a four-chambered heart, normal-sized organs, mammary glands, *et cetera*. A natural conclusion to draw would be that the serpent auxiliary to the body of the cerberus (as well as the chimæra) had adapted appropriately, losing the need for cold-blooded temperature regulatory systems. Similar adaptations are found in other reptiles, such as the *Dermochelys coriacea*, the leather-back turtle. There may be a shared ancestry among these reptiles, suggesting that the bloodlines are vast and still flourishing in regions yet unknown.

PLATE 1

1- Zygomatic arch
2- Condyle of the occipital bone
3- Temporal bone
4- Vertebra
5- 1st–6th thoracic vertebrae
6- Lumbar vertebrae
7- Pelvis
8- Sacrum
9- Caudal vertebra
10- Ribs
11- Phalanges
12- Metatarsal bones
13- Tarsal bones
14- Fibula
15- Tibia
16- Femur
17- Ribs
18- Process of the ulna
19- Radius
20- Ulna
21- Carpal bones
22- Metacarpal bones
23- Phalanges
24- Humerus
25- Scapula
26- Mandible
27- Incisival bone
28- Nasal bone

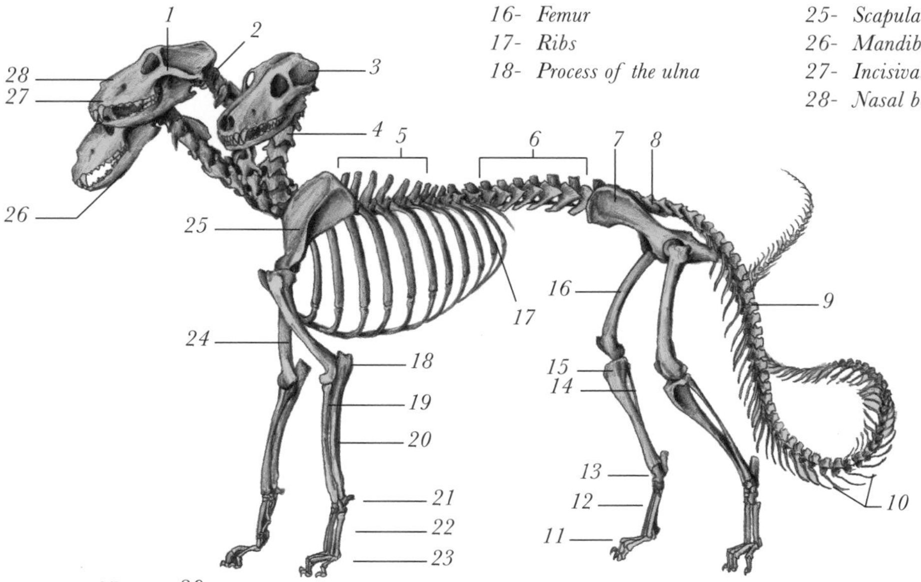

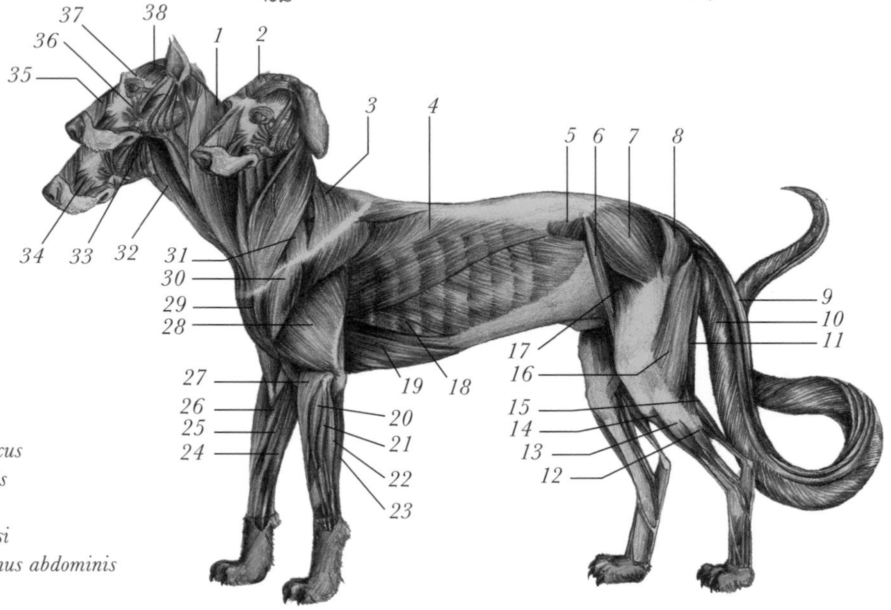

PLATE 2

1- Brachiocephalicus
2- Frontoscutularis
3- Trapezius
4- Latissimus dorsi
5- Obliquus internus abdominis
6- Sartorius
7- Gluteus medius
8- Gluteus superficialis
9- Longissimus dorsi
10- Scutali-interscutali complex
11- Semitendinosus
12- Flexor hallucis longus
13- Peroneus longus
14- Extensor digitorum longus
15- Triceps surae
16- Biceps femoris
17- Tensor fasciae latae
18- Intercostalis externus
19- Pectoralis profundus
20- Extensor digitorum communis
21- Extensor digitorum lateralis
22- Extensor carpi ulnaris
23- Flexor carpi ulnaris
24- Flexor carpi ulnaris
25- Flexor carpi radialis
26- Pronator teres
27- Brachioradialis
28- Triceps brachii
29- Clavicular tendinosus septum
30- Deltoideus
31- Omotransversarius
32- Sternohyoideus
33- Zygomatic cutaneous
34- Caninus
35- Levator nasolabialis
36- Malaris
37- Orbicularis oculi
38- Temporalis

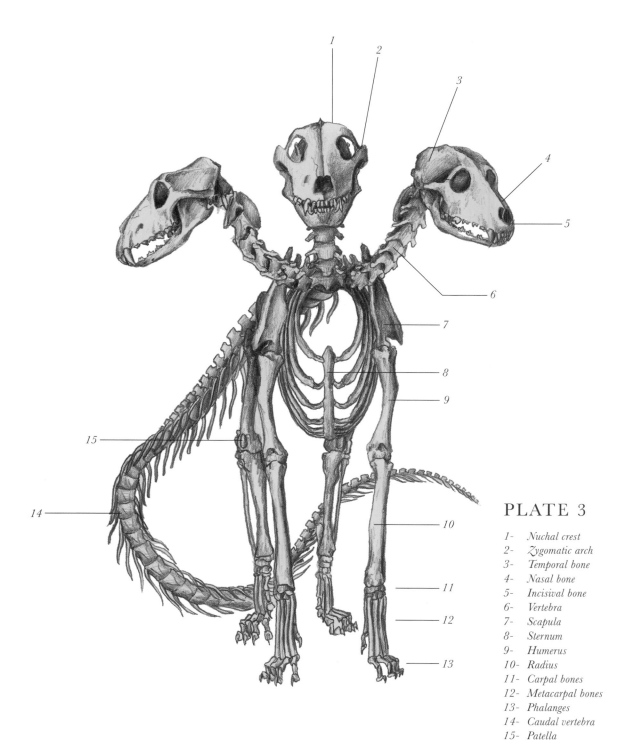

PLATE 3

1- *Nuchal crest*
2- *Zygomatic arch*
3- *Temporal bone*
4- *Nasal bone*
5- *Incisival bone*
6- *Vertebra*
7- *Scapula*
8- *Sternum*
9- *Humerus*
10- *Radius*
11- *Carpal bones*
12- *Metacarpal bones*
13- *Phalanges*
14- *Caudal vertebra*
15- *Patella*

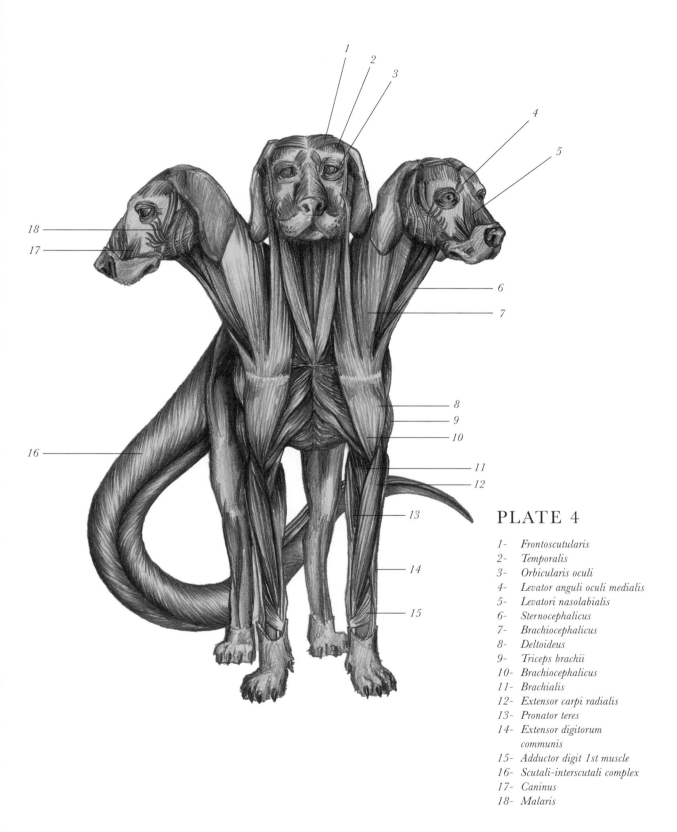

PLATE 4

1- *Frontoscutularis*
2- *Temporalis*
3- *Orbicularis oculi*
4- *Levator anguli oculi medialis*
5- *Levatori nasolabialis*
6- *Sternocephalicus*
7- *Brachiocephalicus*
8- *Deltoideus*
9- *Triceps brachii*
10- *Brachiocephalicus*
11- *Brachialis*
12- *Extensor carpi radialis*
13- *Pronator teres*
14- *Extensor digitorum communis*
15- *Adductor digit 1st muscle*
16- *Scutali-interscutali complex*
17- *Caninus*
18- *Malaris*

CANIS HADES

135

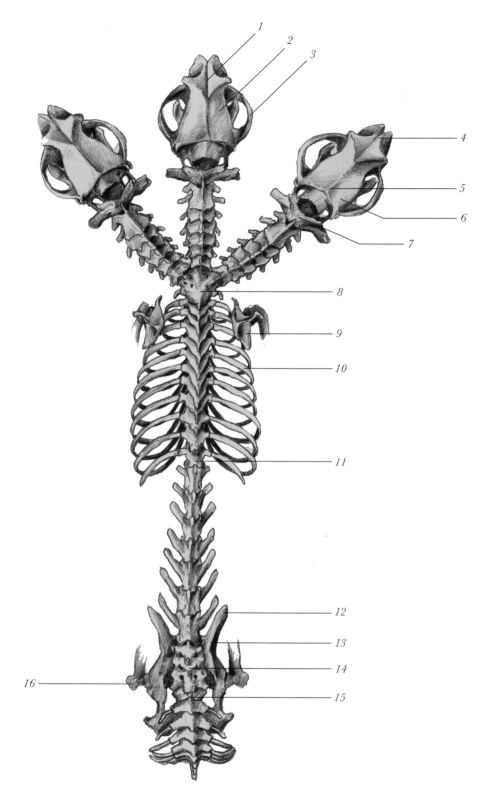

PLATE 5

1- *Frontal bone*
2- *Parietal bone*
3- *Zygomatic arch*
4- *Nasal bone*
5- *Occipital bone*
6- *Temporal bone*
7- *1st cervical vertebra*
8- *Trithoracic vertebra*
9- *Scapula*
10- *Ribs*
11- *12th thoracic vertebra*
12- *Tuber coxae*
13- *Pelvis*
14- *Sacrum*
15- *1st caudal vertebra*
16- *Trochanter major*

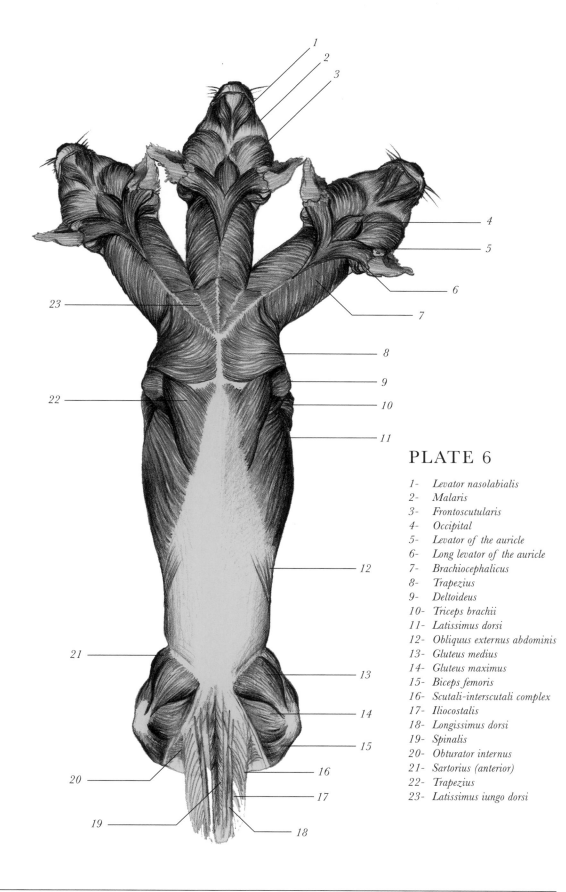

PLATE 6

1- *Levator nasolabialis*
2- *Malaris*
3- *Frontoscutularis*
4- *Occipital*
5- *Levator of the auricle*
6- *Long levator of the auricle*
7- *Brachiocephalicus*
8- *Trapezius*
9- *Deltoideus*
10- *Triceps brachii*
11- *Latissimus dorsi*
12- *Obliquus externus abdominis*
13- *Gluteus medius*
14- *Gluteus maximus*
15- *Biceps femoris*
16- *Scutali-interscutali complex*
17- *Iliocostalis*
18- *Longissimus dorsi*
19- *Spinalis*
20- *Obturator internus*
21- *Sartorius (anterior)*
22- *Trapezius*
23- *Latissimus iungo dorsi*

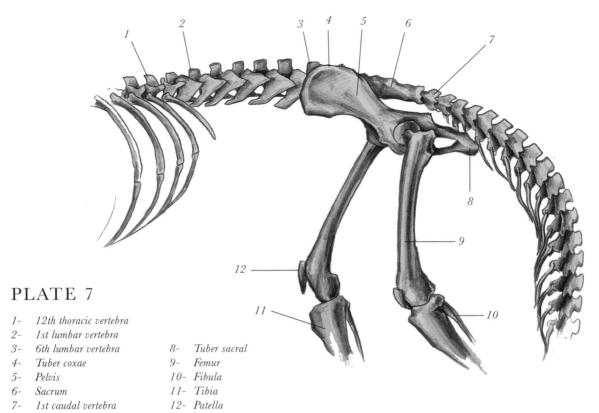

PLATE 7

1- *12th thoracic vertebra*
2- *1st lumbar vertebra*
3- *6th lumbar vertebra*
4- *Tuber coxae*
5- *Pelvis*
6- *Sacrum*
7- *1st caudal vertebra*
8- *Tuber sacral*
9- *Femur*
10- *Fibula*
11- *Tibia*
12- *Patella*

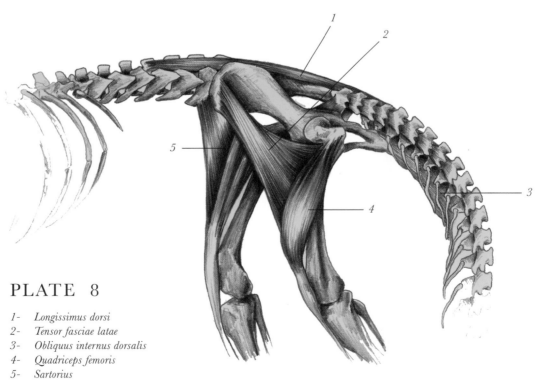

PLATE 8

1- *Longissimus dorsi*
2- *Tensor fasciae latae*
3- *Obliquus internus dorsalis*
4- *Quadriceps femoris*
5- *Sartorius*

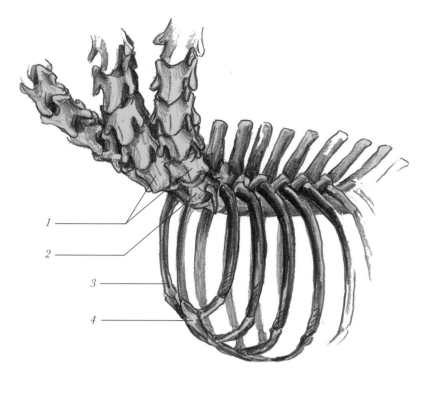

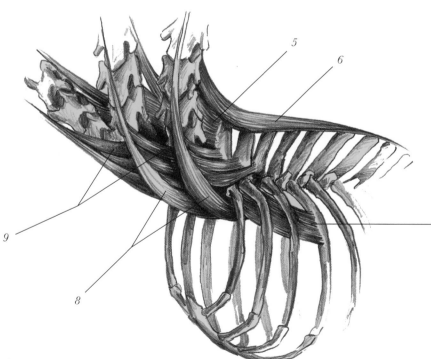

PLATES
9 & 10

1- *7th cervical vertebra*
2- *Trithoracic vertebra*
3- *Ribs*
4- *Sternum*
5- *Semispinalis*
6- *Longissimus dorsi*
7- *Intercostalis internus*
8- *Vertebralcostalis longus*
9- *Serratus ventralis cervicis*

Creating the pegasus was a massive undertaking; it is easily the largest of Dr. Black's creations. He had to design an elaborate hoist-and-pulley system just to move the animal to his operating table. More rigging would be needed to support the creature in its desired posture while on display (it was likely in the same position as was drawn at right).

Months of labor used to construct wings that can never work. I have sewn the muscle carefully to their respective locations; I have taken care with the nerves and skin and all of the fibers of the tissues of the beast's flesh ... but it does not live. I do this, only to show that it could have and once did live.

—Spencer Black

PEGASUS GORGONIS

KINGDOM	*Animalia*	FAMILY	*Equialatus*
PHYLUM	*Vertebrata*	GENUS	*Pegasus*
CLASS	*Gorgonis*	SPECIES	*Pegasus gorgonis*
ORDER	*Perissodactyla*		

FAMED FOR ITS ASCENT to Mount Olympus, the pegasus has inspired many tales of wonderment.

The size and breadth of the animal's wings afford it a greater capacity for flight than might seem possible; certainly the riddle is simple once one peers beyond the veil of the flesh. The air sacs throughout the animal's body would have to be more than twice (by measure of proportion) the size of any bird's, thus allowing tremendous breathing potential. This would be an evolutionary necessity.

The muscles governing the wings were likely very large. If given the opportunity to view genuine pegasus cells under a microscope, I believe we would unravel the secret of their extraordinary strength. These types of cells are not absent from human muscle tissue; they are merely less active. If human cells could be trained to perform with the same functionality as those of the pegasus, then all would marvel at the greatness achievable by man.

The skeletal structure of the animal will seem familiar to any anatomist familiar with the *Aves* and *Equus* forms. Surprisingly, there is no structural deviance from the horse or from the wing structure typical of a common bird. I speculate that this could be quite different among different species of this family.

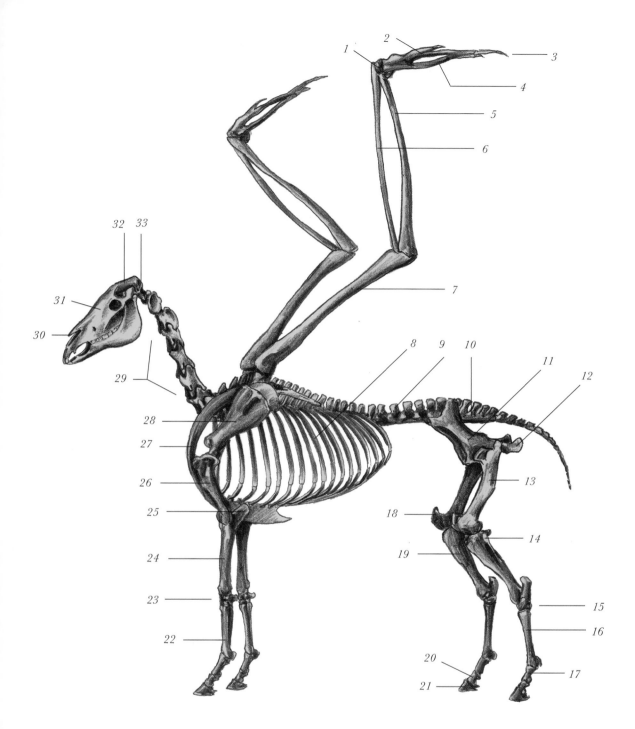

PLATE 1

1- Radial carpal bone
2- 1st finger
3- Phalanges
4- Carpometacarpus
5- Ulna
6- Radius
7- Humerus

8- Ribs
9- Vertebra
10- Sacrum
11- Pelvis
12- Ischium
13- Femur
14- Fibula
15- Tarsal bones
16- 3rd metatarsal bone

17- Proximal phalanx (pastern)
18- Patella
19- Tibia
20- Middle phalanx (coronet)
21- Distal phalanx (coffin bone)
22- 3rd metacarpal bone
23- Carpal bone
24- Radius
25- Olecranon

26- Humerus
27- Furculum
28- Scapula
29- Cervical vertebrae
30- Nasal bone
31- Maxilla
32- Parietal bone
33- Occipital condyle

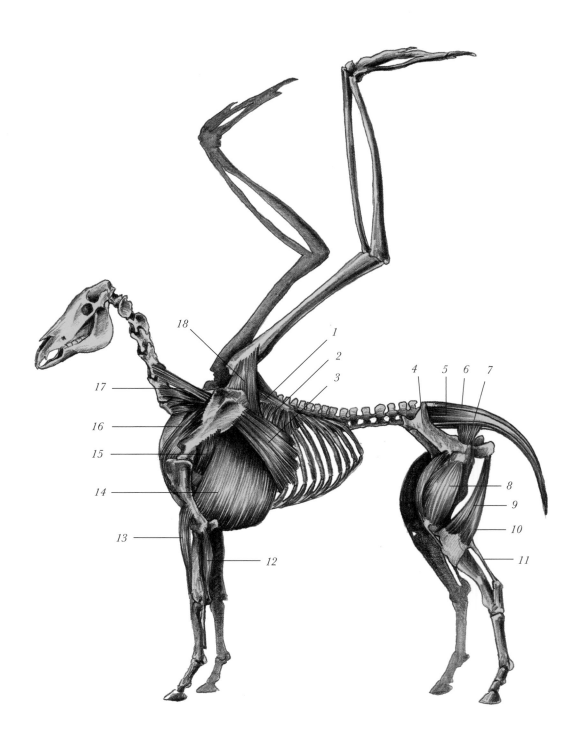

PLATE 2

1- *Scapulohumeralis caudalis*
2- *Serratus dorsalis*
3- *Serratus ventralis thoracis*
4- *Pelvis*
5- *Long levator of the tail*

6- *Short levator of the tail*
7- *Adductor of the tail*
8- *Quadriceps femoris*
9- *Semimembranosus*
10- *Biceps femoris*
11- *Flexor digitorum superficialis*
12- *Extensor carpi ulnaris*

13- *Extensor carpi radialis*
14- *Pectoralis thoracis*
15- *Teres major*
16- *Scapular portion of the pectoralis minor*
17- *Serratus ventralis cervicis*
18- *Pectoralis thoracis*

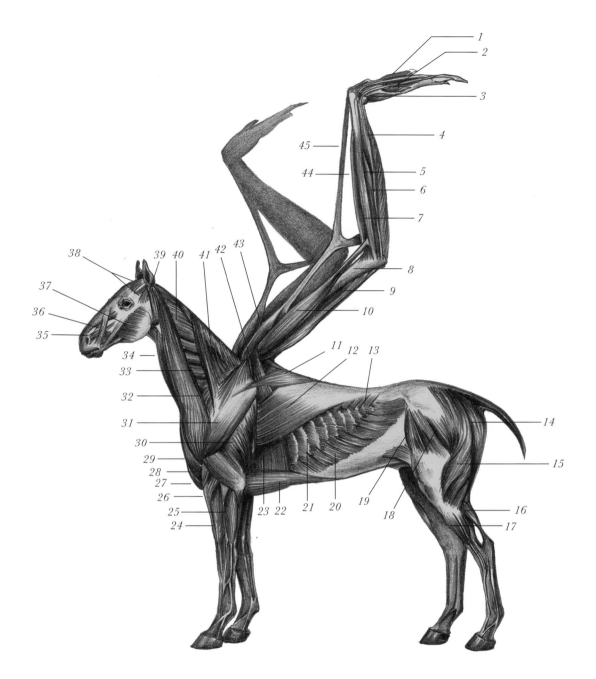

PLATE 3

1- *Adductor alulae*
2- *Interosseus ventralis*
3- *Ulnimetacarpalis dorsalis*
4- *Flexor carpi ulnaris*
5- *Flexor digitorum profundus*
6- *Flexor digitorum superficialis*
7- *Pronator superficialis*
8- *Humerus*
9- *Triceps brachii*
10- *Biceps brachii*

11- *Trapezius muscle*
12- *Latissimus dorsi*
13- *Serratus dorsalis*
14- *Semitendinosus*
15- *Biceps femoris*
16- *Gastrocnemius muscle*
17- *Extensor digitorum longus*
18- *Gluteus maximus*
19- *Fascia latae*
20- *Obliquus externus abdominis*
21- *Intercostalis externus*
22- *Pectoralis profundus*
23- *Pectoralis thoracis*

24- *Extensor digitorum
    communis*
25- *Extensor carpi ulnaris*
26- *Extensor carpi radialis*
27- *Pectoralis major*
28- *Brachialis internus*
29- *Biceps brachii*
30- *Triceps brachii*
31- *Deltoideus*
32- *Supraspinatus*
33- *Serratus ventralis cervicis*
34- *Sternomandibularis*
35- *Caninus muscle*

36- *Levator nasolabialis*
37- *Masseter*
38- *Scutularis muscles*
39- *Parotideoauricularis*
40- *Splenius*
41- *Trapezius muscle*
42- *Pectoralis thoracis*
43- *Tensor propatagialis*
44- *Extensor metacarpi radialis*
45- *Tensor propatagialis long
    tendon*

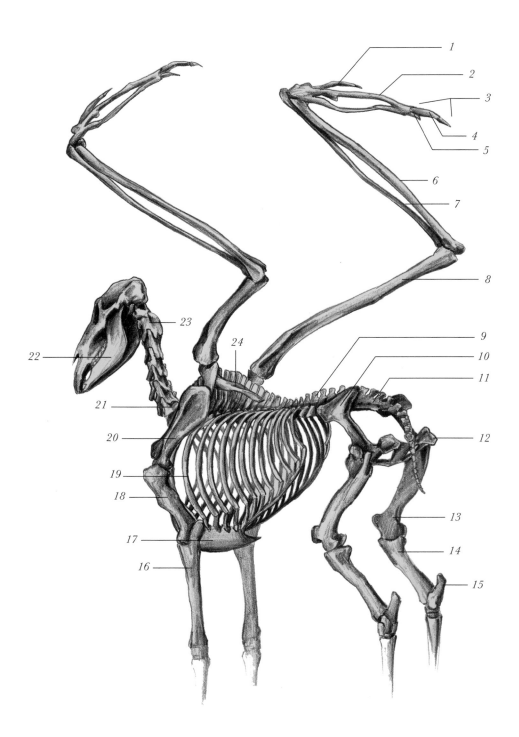

PLATE 4

1- 1st finger
2- Carpometacarpus
3- Phalanges
4- 2nd finger
5- 3rd finger

6- Ulna
7- Radius
8- Humerus
9- Vertebra
10- Pelvis
11- Sacrum
12- Tuber ischiadicum

13- Femur
14- Tibia
15- Tuber calcanei
16- Radius
17- Keel of the sternum
18- Humerus
19- Ribs

20- Scapula
21- 7th cervical vertebra
22- Mandibula
23- 1st cervical vertebra
24- Dorsal scapula

PEGASUS GORGONIS

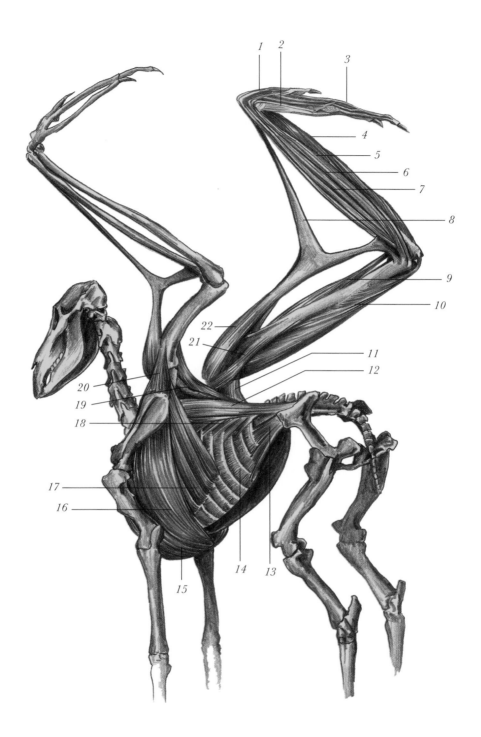

PLATE 5

1- *Adductor alulae*
2- *Ulnimetacarpalis dorsalis*
3- *Extensor longus digiti majoris*
4- *Flexor carpi ulnaris*

5- *Ectepicondyloulnaris*
6- *Extensor metacarpi ulnaris*
7- *Extensor digitorum communis*
8- *Tensor propatagialis (long tendon)*
9- *Biceps brachii*

10- *Triceps brachii*
11- *Latissimus dorsi caudalis*
12- *Longissimus dorsi*
13- *Obliquus abdominis internus*
14- *Intercostalis*
15- *Pectoralis minor*
16- *Thoracic serratus anterior*

17- *Pectoralis thoracis*
18- *Serratus posterior*
19- *Scapulohumeralis caudalis*
20- *Biceps slip*
21- *Deltoid major*
22- *Tensor propatagialis*

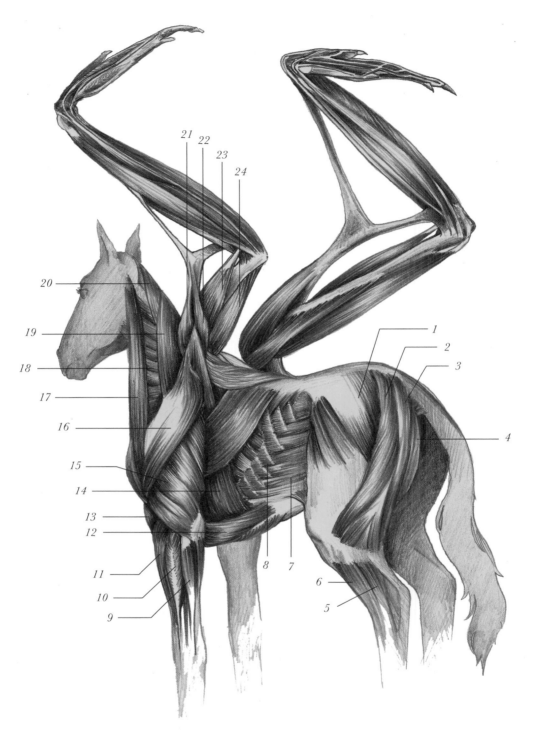

PLATE 6

1- *Fascia glutaea*
2- *Biceps femoris*
3- *Semitendinosus*
4- *Semimembranosus*
5- *Extensor digitorum pedis lateralis*
6- *Extensor digitorum longus*
7- *Obliquus internus*
8- *Intercostalis*
9- *Extensor carpi ulnaris*
10- *Extensor digitorum communis*
11- *Extensor carpi radialis*
12- *Pectoralis minor*
13- *Brachialis internus*
14- *Pectoralis thoracis*
15- *Triceps brachii*
16- *Deltoideus*
17- *Brachiocephalicus*
18- *Serratus ventralis cervicis*
19- *Trapezius muscle*
20- *Splenius*
21- *Tensor propatagialis*
22- *Biceps slip*
23- *Biceps brachii*
24- *Triceps brachii*

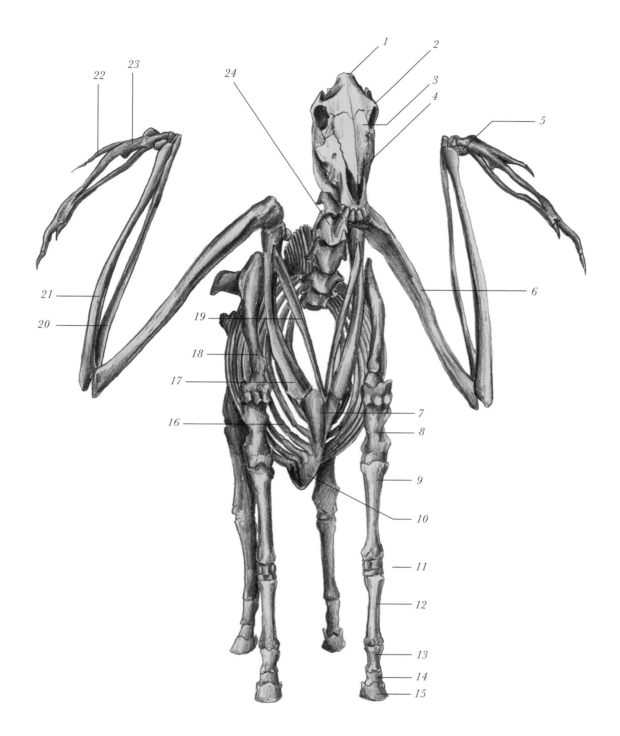

PLATE 7

1- Nuchal crest
2- Frontal bone
3- Maxilla
4- Nasal bone
5- Ulnar carpal

6- Humerus
7- Sternum
8- Humerus
9- Radius
10- Keel of sternum
11- Carpal bones
12- 3rd metacarpal bones

13- Proximal phalanx
14- Middle phalanx
15- Distal phalanx
16- Rib
17- Coracoid
18- Scapula
19- Furculum

20- Radius
21- Ulna
22- 1st finger
23- Carpometacarpus
24- Vertebra

PEGASUS GORGONIS

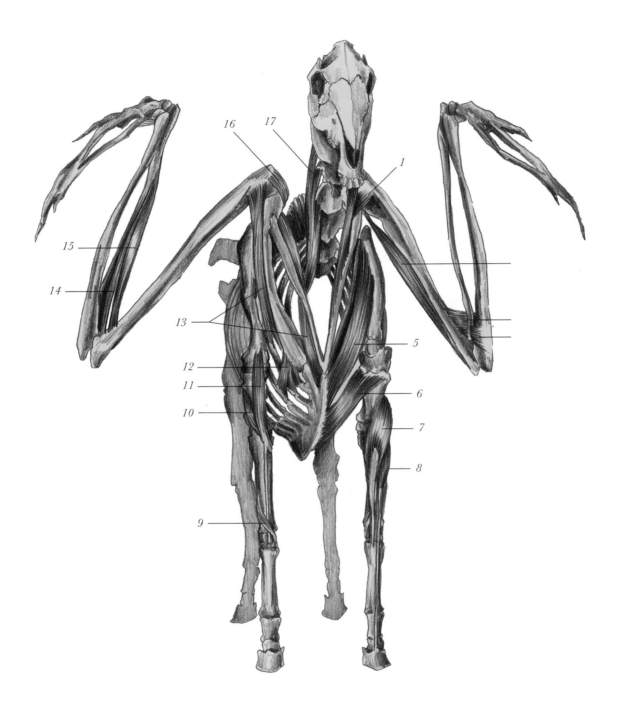

PLATE 8

1- Teres minor
2- Triceps brachii
3- Brachialis
4- Anconeus
5- Sternalpectoralis

6- Pectoralis transversus minor
7- Extensor carpi raadialis
8- Extensor digitorum
   communis
9- Adductor pollicis longus
10- Brachialis internus
11- Biceps brachii

12- Coracoserratus anterior
13- Pectoralis thoracis minor
14- Pronator profundus
15- Pronator superficialis
16- Supraspinatus
17- Longus capitis

PEGASUS GORGONIS

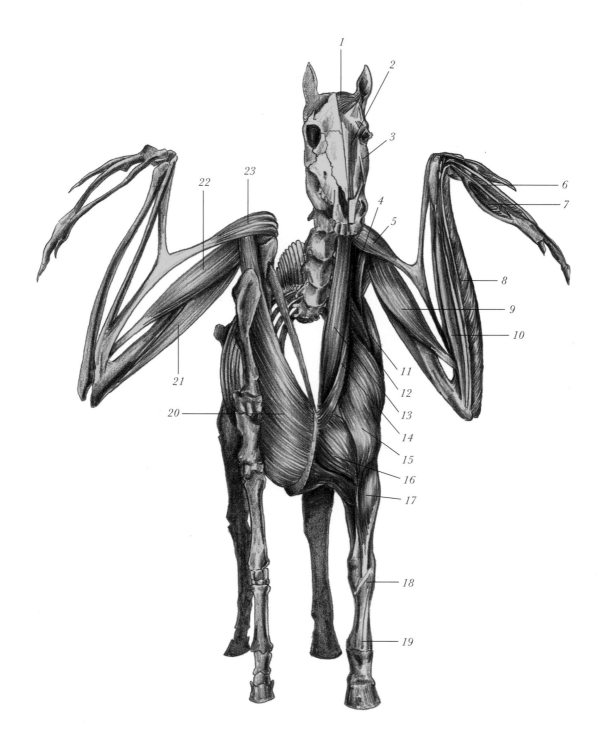

PLATE 9

1- *Scutularis*
2- *Levator nasolabialis*
3- *Masseter*
4- *Pectoralis major*
5- *Tensor propatagialis*
6- *Flexor digitorum superficialis*

7- *Interosseus ventralis*
8- *Flexor carpi ulnaris*
9- *Biceps brachii*
10- *Pronator superficialis*
11- *Trapezius*
12- *Supraspinatus*
13- *Cleidomastoideus*
14- *Cervical subcutaneous*

15- *Brachiocephalicus*
16- *Pectoralis major*
17- *Extensor carpi radialis*
18- *Adductor pollicis longus*
19- *Extensor digitorum communis*
20- *Pectoralis thoracis*
21- *Triceps brachii*

22- *Biceps brachii*
23- *Tensor propatagialis*

THE EASTERN DRAGON IS CERTAINLY ONE OF DR. BLACK'S MOST PLAUSIBLE CREATIONS. HE BELIEVED THAT THE CREATURE—AND MANY LIKE IT—STILL EXIST. HE DESCRIBED THE DRAGON AS A SORT OF LARGE AMPHIBIAN, ANATOMICALLY SIMILAR TO OTHER CREATURES IN ITS CLASS. HE BELIEVED THAT THE DRAGON WAS ONE OF THE WORLD'S GREATEST BEASTS, HAVING NO PREDATORS AND NO GEOGRAPHICAL BOUNDARIES.

INTERESTINGLY, DR. BLACK MENTIONS THE WESTERN (FIRE-BREATHING) VARIETY OF DRAGON IN HIS NOTES. THIS REFLECTS HIS WILLINGNESS TO CONSIDER ALL POSSIBILITIES OF LIFE, NO MATTER HOW FAR-FETCHED THEY MIGHT SEEM.

DRACONIS ORIENTIS

KINGDOM	*Animalia*	**FAMILY**	*Monsdraconis*
PHYLUM	*Vertebrata*	**GENUS**	*Draconis*
CLASS	*Amphibia*	**SPECIES**	*Draconis orientis*
ORDER	*Caudata*		

THIS SPECIMEN WAS DISCOVERED in an old monastery on the island of Nakanotorishima, east of Japan. I was the only one among my companions who believed in its authenticity. I purchased the remains, giving the impression it was *nothing* more than a large serpent, and indeed it really isn't much more than that. It measures forty feet in length, and though I had only partial skeletal remains, I reconstructed the image of this impressive and august animal. Its size, spine protrusions, clearly advanced claws, and defensive capabilities would have lent it a great advantage in its surroundings.

Other dragons, especially the Western variety, are possible ancient ancestors, though I believe the relationship is likely to be distant. With its wings and phosphorous breath, the Western dragon seems more closely related to the leviathan or the hydra than the Eastern dragon shown here. However, since I have not studied the Western species as of yet, I am unable to scientifically confirm this assertion.

The legends of the Far East offer elaborate and thoughtful descriptions of the area's native dragons, suggesting that the authors had an intimate knowledge of the species. Like many of the smaller varieties of serpent, lizard, and amphibian, the dragon must have had many shapes and personalities finely adapted to its specific needs and environment. Certainly many of the species are extinct, but not all; I cannot believe this animal no longer exists. Surely it continues to thrive in the deepest of waters or the darkest of swamps.

DRACONIS ORIENTIS

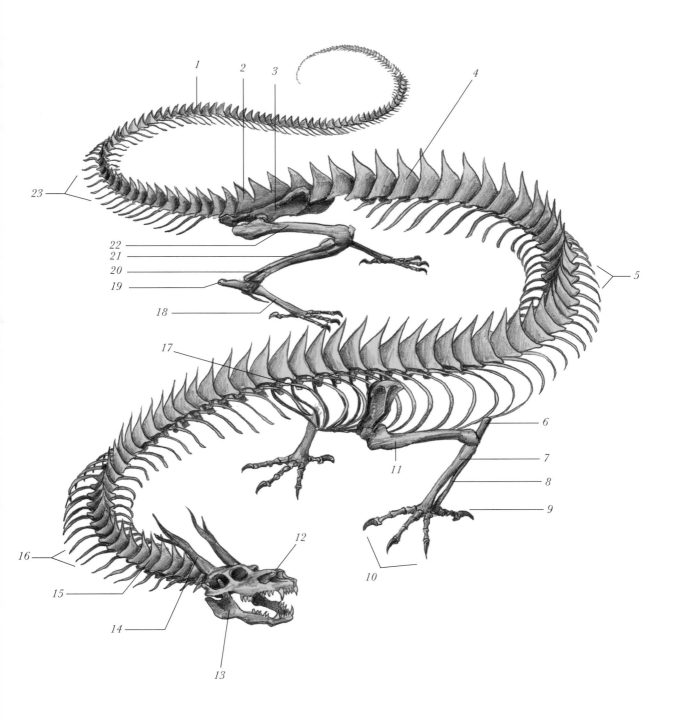

PLATE 1

1- Caudal spinous process
2- Sacrum
3- Pelvis
4- Lumbar spinous process
5- Thoracic ribs

6- Olecranon
7- Radius
8- Ulna
9- Hallux (1st digit)
10- Phalanges
11- Humerus
12- Nasal bone

13- Mandibula
14- Horn
15- Cervical spinous process
16- Cervical ribs
17- 1st thoracic rib
18- Metatarsus
19- Tuber calcanei

20- Tibia
21- Fibula
22- Femur
23- Caudal ribs

PLATE 2

1- Tail
2- Tensor fasciae latae
3- Sartorius
4- Iliocostalis
5- Scutali-interscutali complex
6- Longissimus dorsi
7- Latissimus dorsi
8- Triceps brachii
9- Extensor digitorum communis
10- Cleidobrachialis
11- Deltoideus
12- Trapezius
13- Pectoralis major
14- Levator nasolabialis
15- Orbicularis oculi
16- Buccinator
17- Masseter
18- Scutali-interscutali complex
19- Iliocostalis
20- Biceps femoris
21- Semitendinosus
22- Semimembranosus
23- Adductors of the tail

DRACONIS ORIENTIS

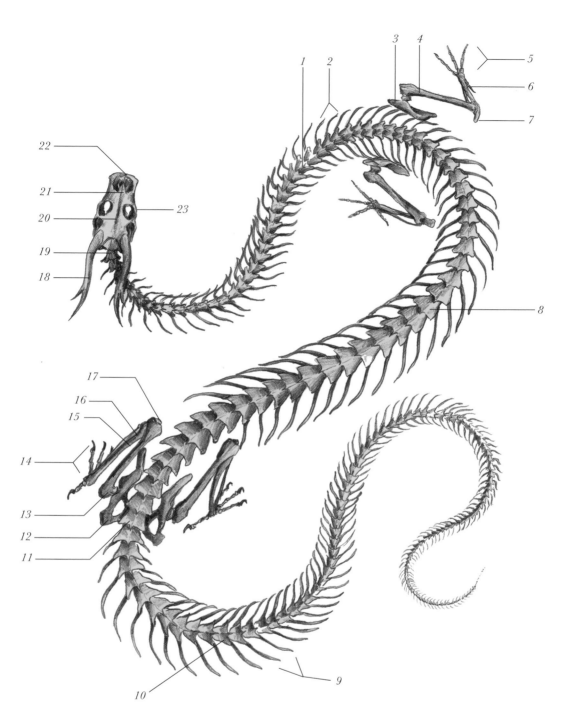

PLATE 3

1- *Cervical spinous process*
2- *Cervical ribs*
3- *Scapula*
4- *Humerus*
5- *Phalanges*
6- *Radius*

7- *Olecranon*
8- *Thoracic spinous process*
9- *Caudal ribs*
10- *Caudal spinous process*
11- *Sacrum*
12- *Pelvis*
13- *Femur*
14- *Phalanges*

15- *Tibia*
16- *Fibula*
17- *Patella*
18- *Horn*
19- *1st cervical vertebra (atlas)*
20- *Parietale*
21- *Nasal bone*
22- *Incisival bone*

23- *Zygomatic arch*

DRACONIS ORIENTIS

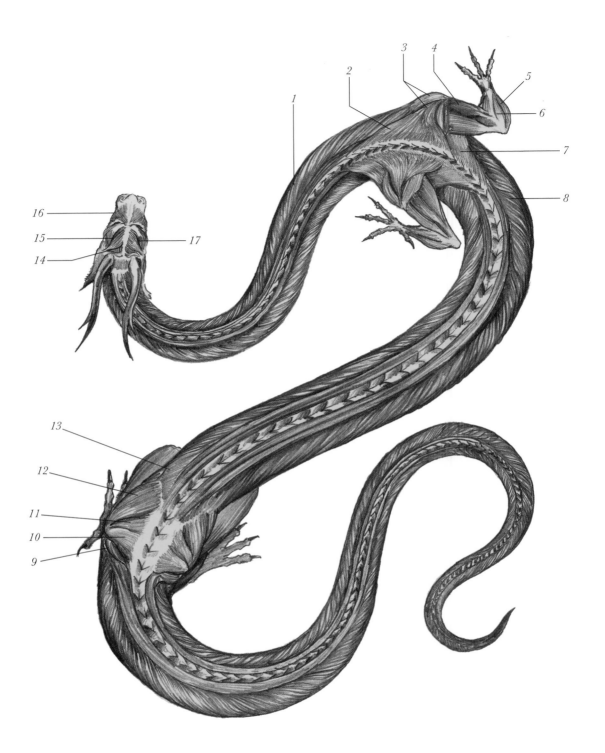

PLATE 4

1- *Iliocostalis*
2- *Trapezius*
3- *Deltoideus*
4- *Triceps brachii*
5- *Extensor carpi ulnaris*

6- *Extensor digitorum lateralis*
7- *Latissimus dorsi*
8- *Iliocostalis*
9- *Semitendinosus*
10- *Adductor cruris*
11- *Gluteus maximus*
12- *Gluteus medius*

13- *Longissimus dorsi*
14- *Levator of the auricle*
15- *Scutularis*
16- *Levator nasolabialis*
17- *Malaris*

DRACONIS ORIENTIS

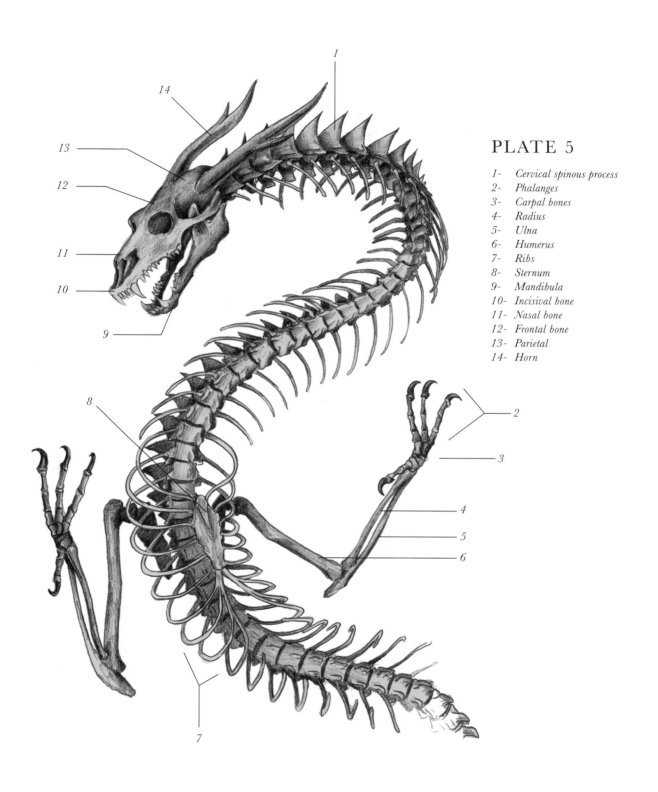

PLATE 5

1- *Cervical spinous process*
2- *Phalanges*
3- *Carpal bones*
4- *Radius*
5- *Ulna*
6- *Humerus*
7- *Ribs*
8- *Sternum*
9- *Mandibula*
10- *Incisival bone*
11- *Nasal bone*
12- *Frontal bone*
13- *Parietal*
14- *Horn*

DRACONIS ORIENTIS

PLATE 6

1- *Longissimus dorsi*
2- *Iliocostalis*
3- *Scutali-interscutali complex*
4- *Pectoralis major*
5- *Deltoideus*
6- *Biceps brachii*
7- *Triceps brachii*
8- *Brachioradialis*
9- *Flexor carpi radialis*
10- *Palmaris longus*
11- *Brachialis*
12- *Abdominis scutali*
13- *Serratus costalis*
14- *Flexor carpi ulnaris*
15- *Adductor digiti 1st longus
    & brevis*
16- *Levator nasolabialis*
17- *Orbicularis oculi*
18- *Temporalis*
19- *Masseter*
20- *Buccinator*
21- *Pterygoideus*

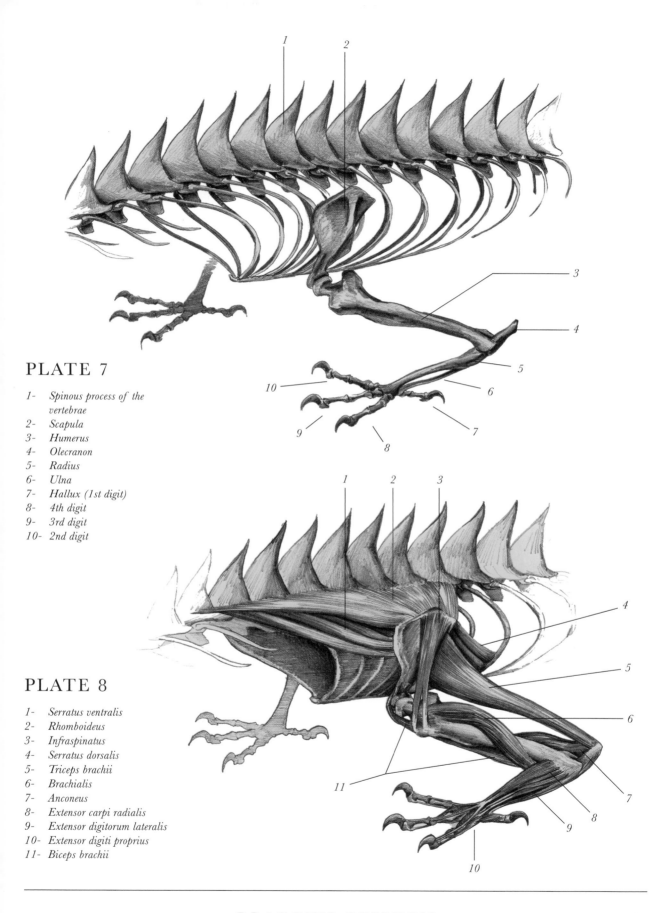

PLATE 7

1- *Spinous process of the vertebrae*
2- *Scapula*
3- *Humerus*
4- *Olecranon*
5- *Radius*
6- *Ulna*
7- *Hallux (1st digit)*
8- *4th digit*
9- *3rd digit*
10- *2nd digit*

PLATE 8

1- *Serratus ventralis*
2- *Rhomboideus*
3- *Infraspinatus*
4- *Serratus dorsalis*
5- *Triceps brachii*
6- *Brachialis*
7- *Anconeus*
8- *Extensor carpi radialis*
9- *Extensor digitorum lateralis*
10- *Extensor digiti proprius*
11- *Biceps brachii*

DRACONIS ORIENTIS

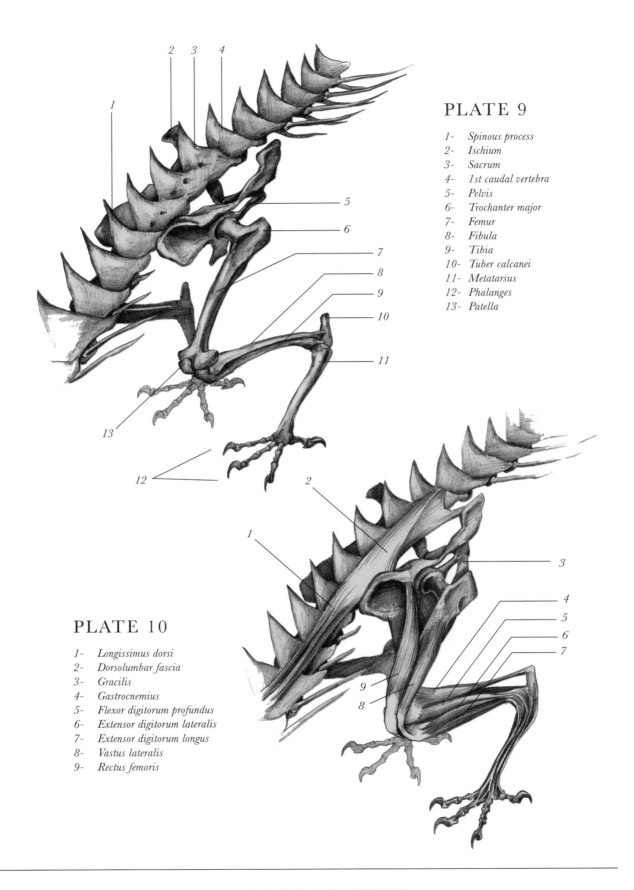

PLATE 9

1- Spinous process
2- Ischium
3- Sacrum
4- 1st caudal vertebra
5- Pelvis
6- Trochanter major
7- Femur
8- Fibula
9- Tibia
10- Tuber calcanei
11- Metatarsus
12- Phalanges
13- Patella

PLATE 10

1- Longissimus dorsi
2- Dorsolumbar fascia
3- Gracilis
4- Gastrocnemius
5- Flexor digitorum profundus
6- Extensor digitorum lateralis
7- Extensor digitorum longus
8- Vastus lateralis
9- Rectus femoris

DRACONIS ORIENTIS

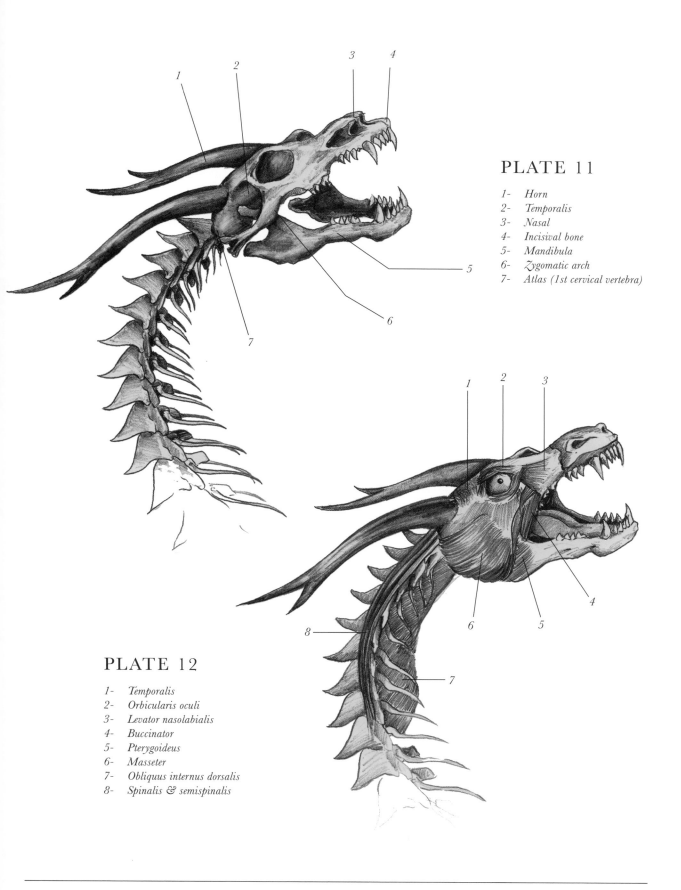

PLATE 11

1- *Horn*
2- *Temporalis*
3- *Nasal*
4- *Incisival bone*
5- *Mandibula*
6- *Zygomatic arch*
7- *Atlas (1st cervical vertebra)*

PLATE 12

1- *Temporalis*
2- *Orbicularis oculi*
3- *Levator nasolabialis*
4- *Buccinator*
5- *Pterygoideus*
6- *Masseter*
7- *Obliquus internus dorsalis*
8- *Spinalis & semispinalis*

Because of the centaur's exceptional weight, Black likely employed the same elaborate pulley system used during the creation of the pegasus. It is believed that most of his taxidermy creations are still in existence, but only hidden away in private collections. Black was considered an excellent taxidermist, and any collector would seek his work, likely at a considerably high price.

Black mentions finding evidence in a small Bulgarian village, but there are no accounts from other archeologists to corroborate these reports.

CENTAURUS
CABALLUS

KINGDOM	*Animalia*	**FAMILY**	*Homoequidæ*
PHYLUM	*Vertebrata*	**GENUS**	*Centaurus*
CLASS	*Mammalia*	**SPECIES**	*Centaurus caballus*
ORDER	*Perissodactyla*		

THE LEGENDS REGARDING these animals are richly colored and decidedly unfavorable. It is possible the centaur was hunted to extinction. Their remains have been found cut into pieces and then ceremonially buried, which suggests they had acquired enemies with a fervor for extravagant punishment. Nevertheless, the centaur prospered long enough to allow for many descendants in its natural history: the *centarus ipotane* (humans with horse feet); *pterocentaur* (winged centaur); *onocentaur* (half man and half bull or ass); and possibly many others.

I acquired the research for my specimen in a small village in Bulgaria, east of Sofia, in the Balkans. There I found a great deal of evidence to suggest that any further excavation and research will bear great and many anthropological fruits. I was unable to homestead in the beautiful countryside for as long as I would have desired. Perhaps one day the research of another scientist will bestow upon the world the secrets of this civilization and the power of the great centaur.

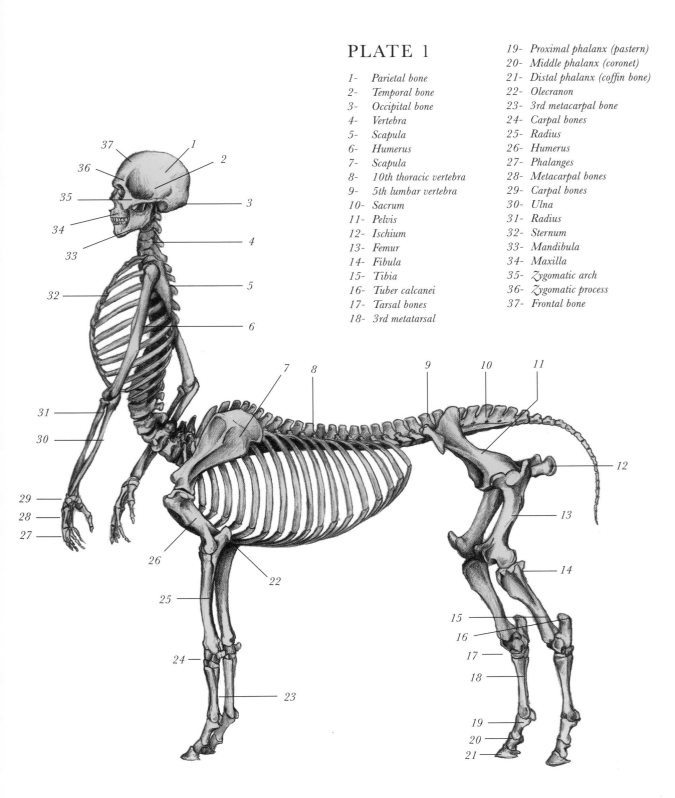

PLATE 1

1- *Parietal bone*
2- *Temporal bone*
3- *Occipital bone*
4- *Vertebra*
5- *Scapula*
6- *Humerus*
7- *Scapula*
8- *10th thoracic vertebra*
9- *5th lumbar vertebra*
10- *Sacrum*
11- *Pelvis*
12- *Ischium*
13- *Femur*
14- *Fibula*
15- *Tibia*
16- *Tuber calcanei*
17- *Tarsal bones*
18- *3rd metatarsal*
19- *Proximal phalanx (pastern)*
20- *Middle phalanx (coronet)*
21- *Distal phalanx (coffin bone)*
22- *Olecranon*
23- *3rd metacarpal bone*
24- *Carpal bones*
25- *Radius*
26- *Humerus*
27- *Phalanges*
28- *Metacarpal bones*
29- *Carpal bones*
30- *Ulna*
31- *Radius*
32- *Sternum*
33- *Mandibula*
34- *Maxilla*
35- *Zygomatic arch*
36- *Zygomatic process*
37- *Frontal bone*

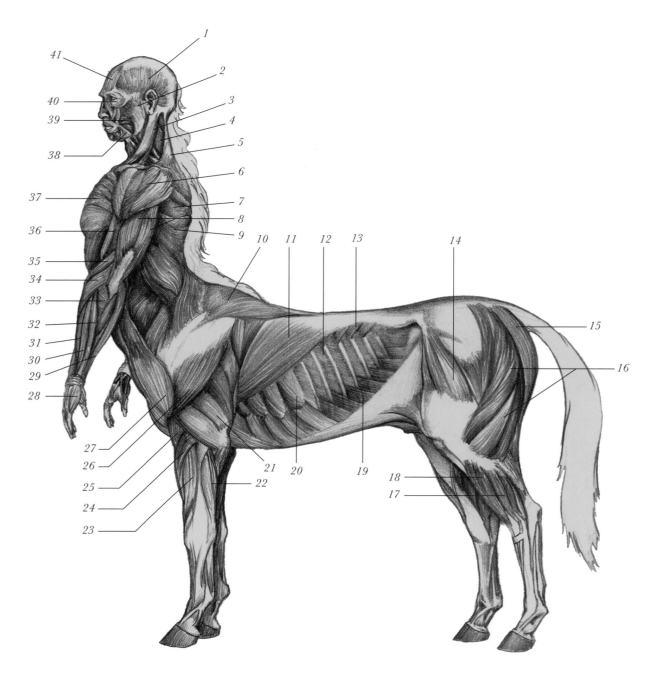

PLATE 2

1- Temporalis
2- Masseter
3- Sternomastoid
4- Levator scapulae
5- Trapezius
6- Deltoid
7- Teres major
8- Triceps brachii
9- Latissimus dorsi
10- Trapezius

11- Latissimus dorsi
12- Intercostalis externus
13- Serratus posterior
14- Tensor fasciae latae
15- Semitendinosus
16- Biceps femoris
17- Extensor digitorum lateralis
18- Tibialis caudalis
19- Obliquus abdominis externus
20- Serratus thoracis
21- Triceps brachii
22- Extensor carpi ulnaris

23- Extensor digitorum communis
24- Extensor carpi radialis
25- Brachialis
26- Deltoid
27- Brachiocephalicus
28- Hypothenar
29- Flexor digitorum sublimis
30- Extensor digitorum communis
31- Extensor carpi radialis brevis

32- Extensor carpi ulnaris
33- Anconeus
34- Extensor carpi radialis
35- Brachioradialis
36- Biceps brachii
37- Pectoralis major
38- Triangularis
39- Risorius
40- Orbicularis oculi
41- Frontalis

CENTAURUS CABALLUS

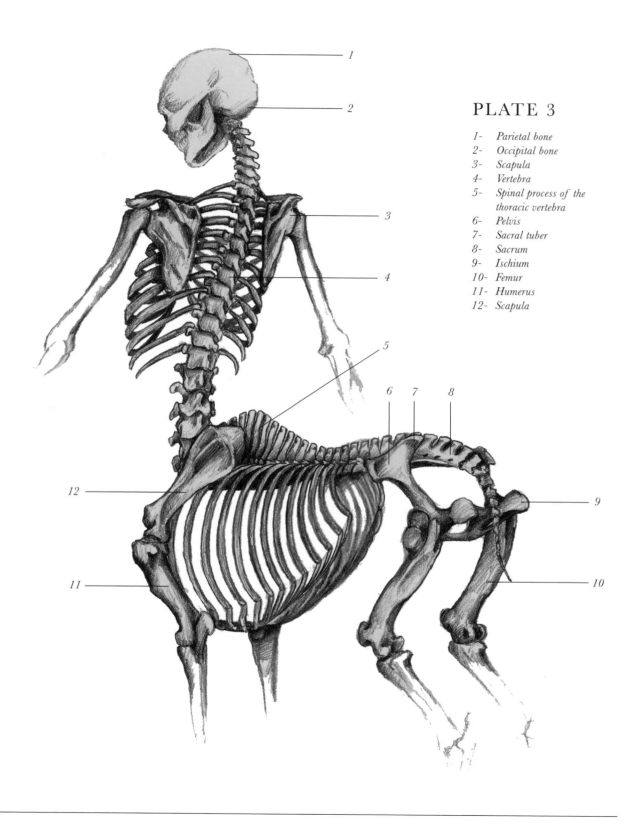

PLATE 3

1- *Parietal bone*
2- *Occipital bone*
3- *Scapula*
4- *Vertebra*
5- *Spinal process of the thoracic vertebra*
6- *Pelvis*
7- *Sacral tuber*
8- *Sacrum*
9- *Ischium*
10- *Femur*
11- *Humerus*
12- *Scapula*

PLATE 4

1- *Sternomastoid*
2- *Trapezius*
3- *Deltoideus*
4- *Triceps brachii*
5- *Latissimus dorsi*
6- *Trapezius*
7- *Latissimus dorsi*
8- *Intercostalis externus*
9- *Tensor fasciae latae*
10- *Gluteus superficialis*
11- *Biceps femoris*
12- *Semitendinosus*
13- *Semimembranosus*
14- *Gracilis*
15- *Extensor digitorum longus*
16- *Obliquus externus abdominis*
17- *Extensor carpi radialis*
18- *Tricpes brachii*
19- *Serratus ventralis*
20- *Deltoideus*
21- *Brachiocephalicus*
22- *Sternogluteus*
23- *Obliquus externus abdominis*
24- *Teres major*
25- *Teres minor*
26- *Infraspinatus*

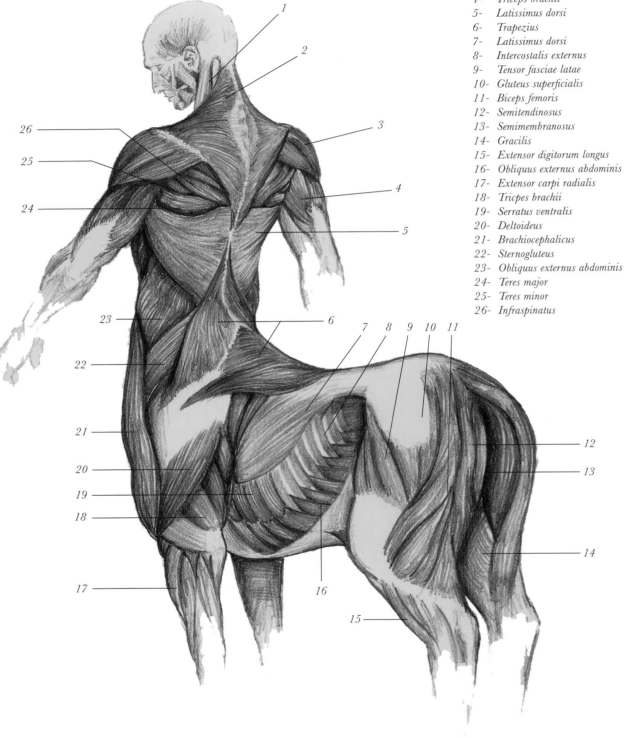

CENTAURUS CABALLUS

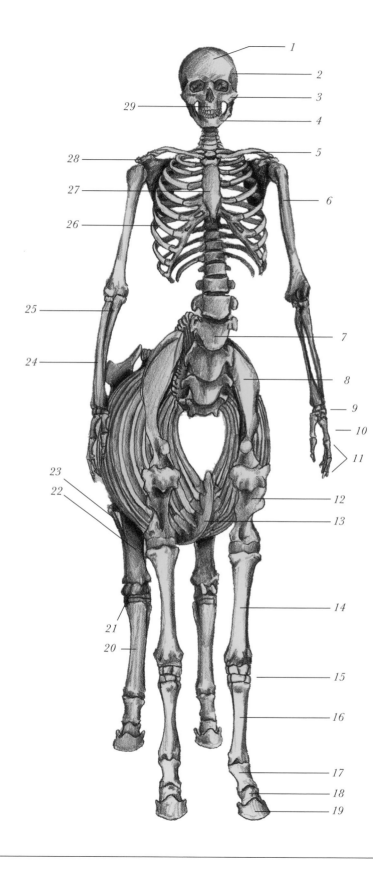

PLATE 5

1- *Frontal bone*
2- *Temporal bone*
3- *Zygomatic arch*
4- *Mandibula*
5- *Clavicle*
6- *Humerus*
7- *Lumbo-cervical vertebra*
8- *Scapula*
9- *Carpal bones*
10- *Metacarpal bones*
11- *Phalanges*
12- *Humerus*
13- *Sternum*
14- *Radis*
15- *Carpal bones*
16- *3rd metacarpal bone*
17- *Proximal phalanx*
18- *Middle phalanx*
19- *Distal phalanx*
20- *3rd metatarsal bone*
21- *Tarsal bone*
22- *Tibia*
23- *Fibula*
24- *Radius*
25- *Ulna*
26- *Ribs*
27- *Sternum*
28- *Scapula*
29- *Maxilla*

CENTAURUS CABALLUS

171

PLATE 6

1- *Frontalis muscle*
2- *Orbicularis oculi*
3- *Levator labii superioris*
4- *Depressor anguli oris*
5- *Sternocleidomastoideus*
6- *Deltoideus*
7- *Pectoralis major*
8- *Biceps brachii*
9- *Rectus abdominis*
10- *Brachioradialis*
11- *Extensor carpi radialis*
12- *Sternothoracis*
13- *Lumbo-cervical subcutaneus*
14- *Brachiocephalicus*
15- *Pectoralis major*
16- *Brachialis*
17- *Extensor carpi radialis*
18- *Flexor carpi radialis*
19- *Triceps brachii*
20- *Thenar muscles*
21- *Flexor carpi radialis*
22- *Pronator teres*
23- *Brachialis*
24- *Serratus*
25- *Trapezius*
26- *Orbicularis*

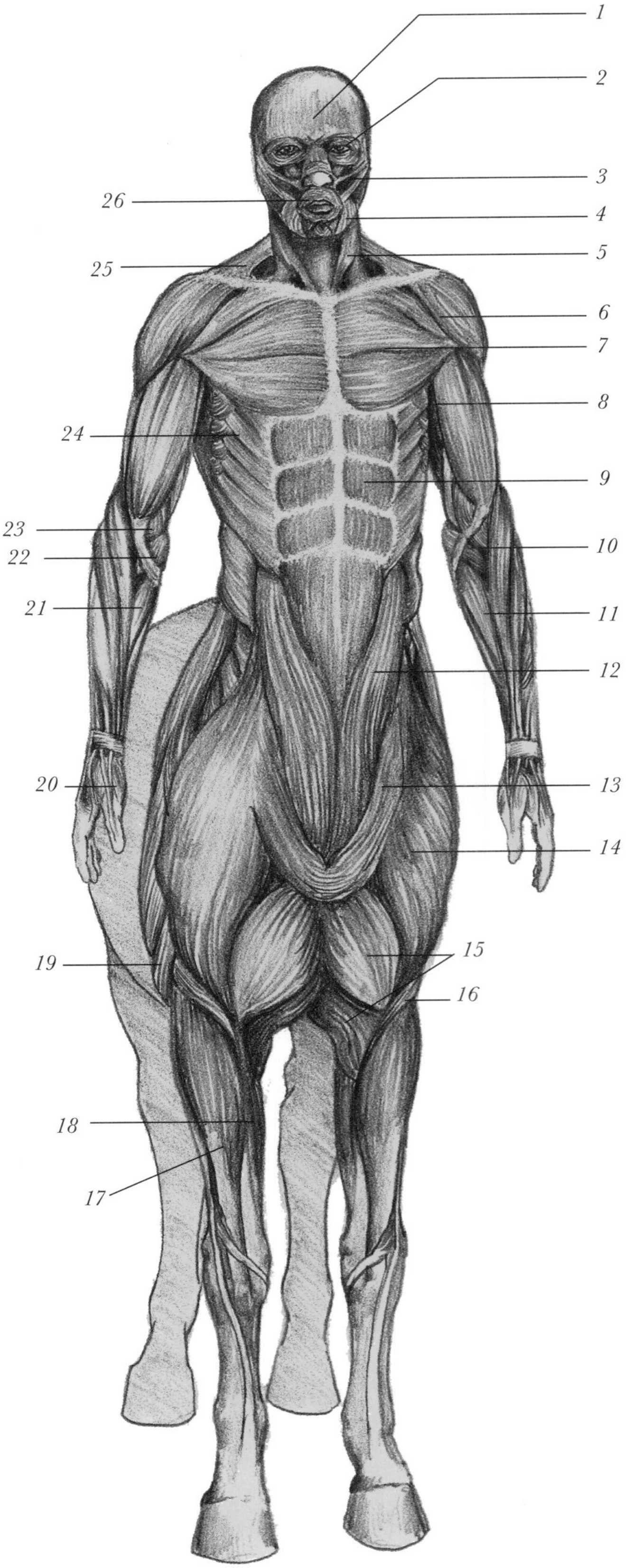

CENTAURUS CABALLUS

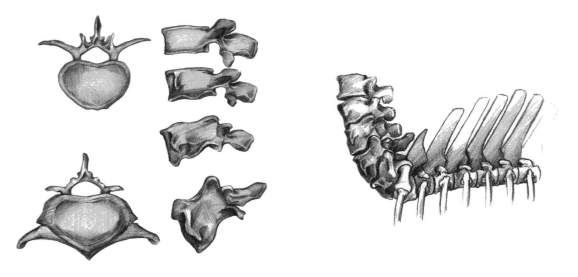

PLATE 7

1- *Obliquus externus abdomins*
2- *Trapezius (see cut-away)*
3- *Serratus dorsalis*
4- *Intercostalis externus*
5- *Obliquus externus abdominis*
6- *Pectoralis profundus*
7- *Serratus ventralis*
8- *Infraspinatus*
9- *Supraspinatus*
10- *Cutaneus collilumborum*
11- *Serratus ventralis*
11a- *Serratus ventralis*
    (see cut-away)
12- *Rectus abdominis*

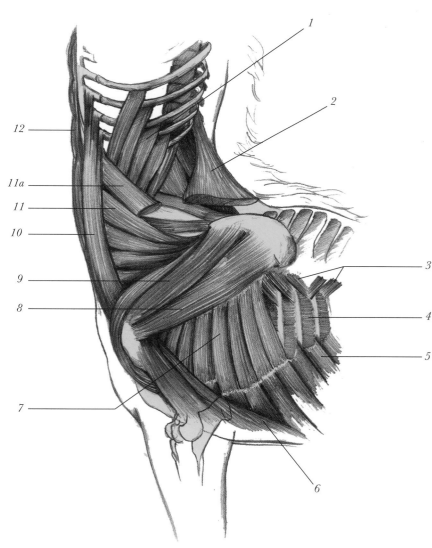

THE HARPY WAS THE CULMINATION OF DR.
BLACK'S ACHIEVEMENTS—HIS GREATEST
DEMONSTRATION OF THE HUMAN FORM
AND ITS CAPACITY FOR SELF-EVOLUTION.
THIS IS EASILY THE LONGEST CHAPTER OF
THE CODEX, WITH MANY ILLUSTRATIONS OF
NOT ONLY THE MUSCULAR AND SKELETAL
SYSTEMS, BUT ALSO THE PHYSIOLOGICAL
AND EVEN THE REPRODUCTIVE SYSTEMS.

HARPY
ERINYES

KINGDOM	*Animalia*	**FAMILY**	*Harpyiadæ*
PHYLUM	*Vertebrata*	**GENUS**	*Harpy*
CLASS	*Mammalatus*	**SPECIES**	*Harpy erinyes*
ORDER	*Harpyiaforme*		

THE HARPY IS THE mother of all wonders. She was once beloved as a beautiful goddess; more recent portrayals depict her as a wretched beast. I suspect this confusion results from observers viewing different species of the harpy family and ignorantly thinking them to be the same. A likeness can readily be made with other similar species: the cherubim, the Boreads, and a host of others. The species that is studied here is one of the ancient ones, quite unlike its larger and more distasteful cousins.

The smaller harpies do not possess the additional limbs characterized in the likeness of human arms; they are more fowl than human. They do maintain what is clearly a human head and neck; a protrusion in the maxilla forms a hard beak-like ridge underneath the lips, both top and bottom. Only the deep teeth remain: molars and wisdom teeth. The incisor and canine groups are replaced with the beak. The surface of the face (*capital* and *submalar* tracks) is cloaked with a fine layering of feathers, making it appear like an ordinary bird's when viewed from a distance.

Like many other birds, the harpy has a sophisticated air circulatory system composed of sacs that assist in cooling and allow uninterrupted flow of air through their lungs. This mechanism grants the animal the ability to breathe continuously, even during exhalation. The sacs also contribute to lowering body heat from the wing extremities and internal organs.

The harpy's reproductive system is similar to that of a bird. She has one active ovary and lays eggs. The size of the eggs would have been quite large, perhaps 17–20 centimeters in diameter, and the time of gestation for the newborn would have been nearly five weeks. The young would exit the shell with the help of an egg tooth (a small rigid spike on the forehead used for breaking the egg, which goes away in its early life).

Possessing both the syrinx and the larynx allowed the dual functions of birdsong and the ability to speak. Nevertheless, no evidence of a harpy language has yet been found. Its vascular system bears no great riddles; there is the presence of a complex array of arterial and venous structures that are not foreign to the practitioner of medicine and anatomy.

Additional notes regarding the physiology: lacking a gizzard but instead having a human stomach and large pancreas, an intestinal tract shorter than a human's and still of a greater length than that of a bird's, a four-chambered heart and particularly large kidneys would allow the harpy to have married the physiological differences of fowl and human in the bosom. I presume its diet would be carnivorous but certainly capable of digesting nearly anything, even if necrotic.

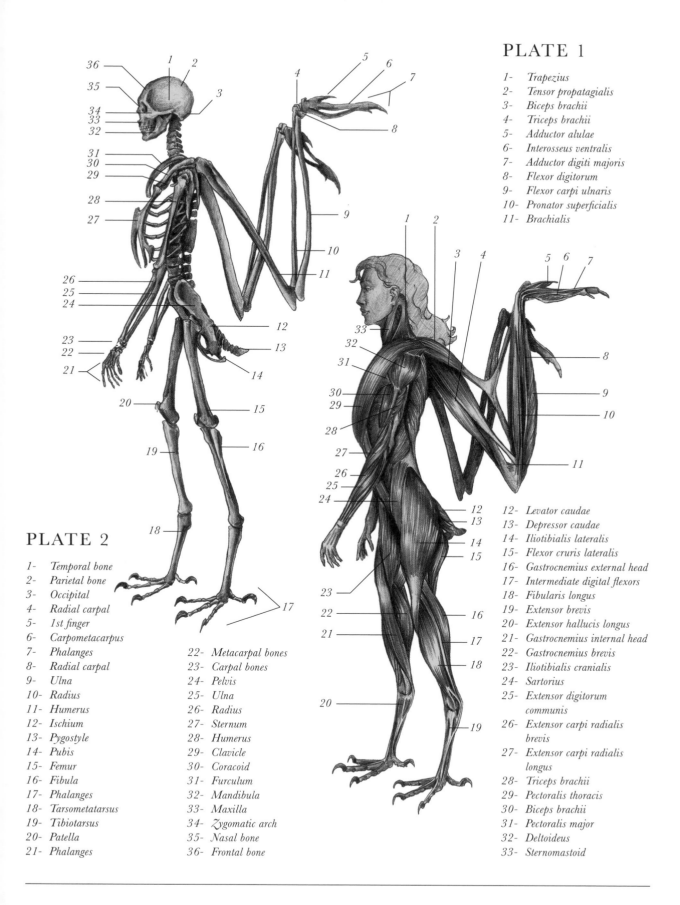

PLATE 1

1- Trapezius
2- Tensor propatagialis
3- Biceps brachii
4- Triceps brachii
5- Adductor alulae
6- Interosseus ventralis
7- Adductor digiti majoris
8- Flexor digitorum
9- Flexor carpi ulnaris
10- Pronator superficialis
11- Brachialis

12- Levator caudae
13- Depressor caudae
14- Iliotibialis lateralis
15- Flexor cruris lateralis
16- Gastrocnemius external head
17- Intermediate digital flexors
18- Fibularis longus
19- Extensor brevis
20- Extensor hallucis longus
21- Gastrocnemius internal head
22- Gastrocnemius brevis
23- Iliotibialis cranialis
24- Sartorius
25- Extensor digitorum communis
26- Extensor carpi radialis brevis
27- Extensor carpi radialis longus
28- Triceps brachii
29- Pectoralis thoracis
30- Biceps brachii
31- Pectoralis major
32- Deltoideus
33- Sternomastoid

PLATE 2

1- Temporal bone
2- Parietal bone
3- Occipital
4- Radial carpal
5- 1st finger
6- Carpometacarpus
7- Phalanges
8- Radial carpal
9- Ulna
10- Radius
11- Humerus
12- Ischium
13- Pygostyle
14- Pubis
15- Femur
16- Fibula
17- Phalanges
18- Tarsometatarsus
19- Tibiotarsus
20- Patella
21- Phalanges

22- Metacarpal bones
23- Carpal bones
24- Pelvis
25- Ulna
26- Radius
27- Sternum
28- Humerus
29- Clavicle
30- Coracoid
31- Furculum
32- Mandibula
33- Maxilla
34- Zygomatic arch
35- Nasal bone
36- Frontal bone

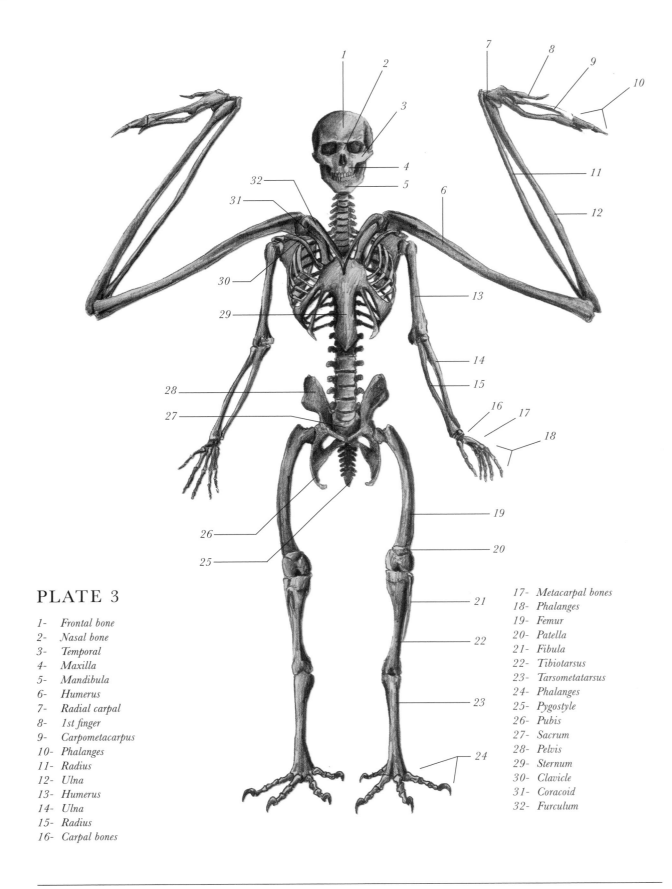

PLATE 3

1- Frontal bone
2- Nasal bone
3- Temporal
4- Maxilla
5- Mandibula
6- Humerus
7- Radial carpal
8- 1st finger
9- Carpometacarpus
10- Phalanges
11- Radius
12- Ulna
13- Humerus
14- Ulna
15- Radius
16- Carpal bones

17- Metacarpal bones
18- Phalanges
19- Femur
20- Patella
21- Fibula
22- Tibiotarsus
23- Tarsometatarsus
24- Phalanges
25- Pygostyle
26- Pubis
27- Sacrum
28- Pelvis
29- Sternum
30- Clavicle
31- Coracoid
32- Furculum

HARPY ERINYES

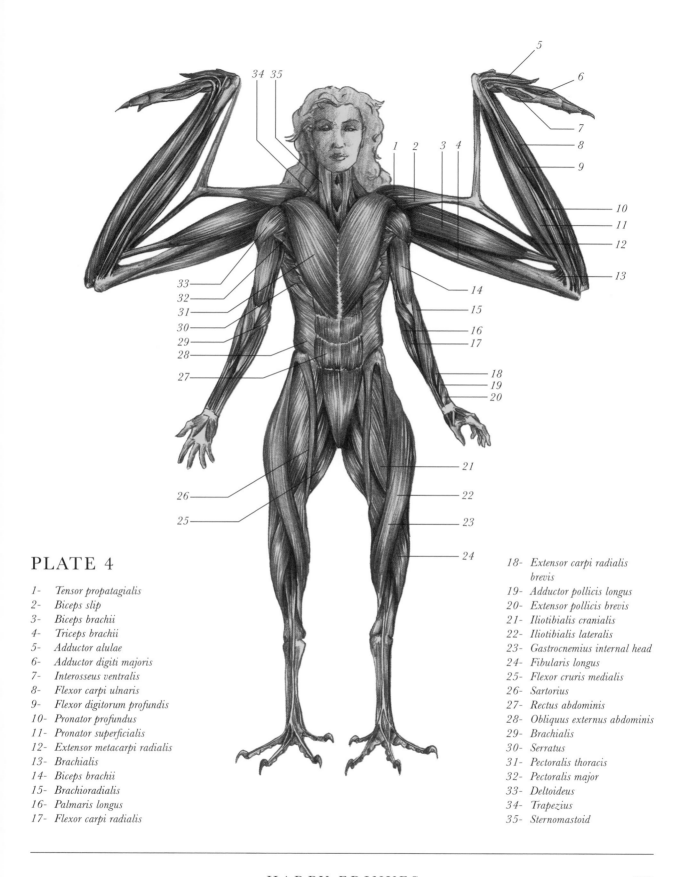

PLATE 4

1- *Tensor propatagialis*
2- *Biceps slip*
3- *Biceps brachii*
4- *Triceps brachii*
5- *Adductor alulae*
6- *Adductor digiti majoris*
7- *Interosseus ventralis*
8- *Flexor carpi ulnaris*
9- *Flexor digitorum profundis*
10- *Pronator profundus*
11- *Pronator superficialis*
12- *Extensor metacarpi radialis*
13- *Brachialis*
14- *Biceps brachii*
15- *Brachioradialis*
16- *Palmaris longus*
17- *Flexor carpi radialis*

18- *Extensor carpi radialis brevis*
19- *Adductor pollicis longus*
20- *Extensor pollicis brevis*
21- *Iliotibialis cranialis*
22- *Iliotibialis lateralis*
23- *Gastrocnemius internal head*
24- *Fibularis longus*
25- *Flexor cruris medialis*
26- *Sartorius*
27- *Rectus abdominis*
28- *Obliquus externus abdominis*
29- *Brachialis*
30- *Serratus*
31- *Pectoralis thoracis*
32- *Pectoralis major*
33- *Deltoideus*
34- *Trapezius*
35- *Sternomastoid*

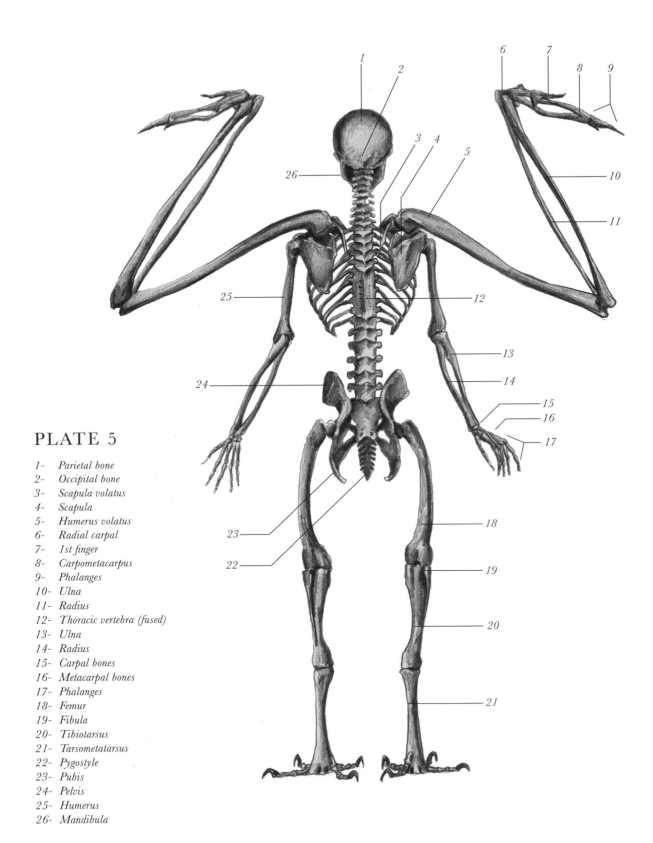

PLATE 5

1- *Parietal bone*
2- *Occipital bone*
3- *Scapula volatus*
4- *Scapula*
5- *Humerus volatus*
6- *Radial carpal*
7- *1st finger*
8- *Carpometacarpus*
9- *Phalanges*
10- *Ulna*
11- *Radius*
12- *Thoracic vertebra (fused)*
13- *Ulna*
14- *Radius*
15- *Carpal bones*
16- *Metacarpal bones*
17- *Phalanges*
18- *Femur*
19- *Fibula*
20- *Tibiotarsus*
21- *Tarsometatarsus*
22- *Pygostyle*
23- *Pubis*
24- *Pelvis*
25- *Humerus*
26- *Mandibula*

HARPY ERINYES

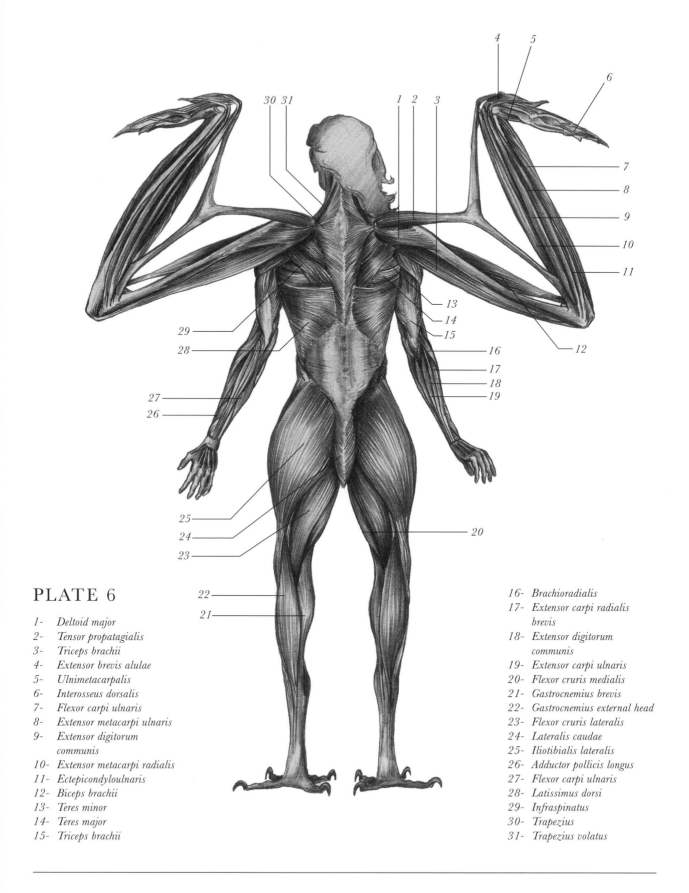

PLATE 6

1- Deltoid major
2- Tensor propatagialis
3- Triceps brachii
4- Extensor brevis alulae
5- Ulnimetacarpalis
6- Interosseus dorsalis
7- Flexor carpi ulnaris
8- Extensor metacarpi ulnaris
9- Extensor digitorum
   communis
10- Extensor metacarpi radialis
11- Ectepicondyloulnaris
12- Biceps brachii
13- Teres minor
14- Teres major
15- Triceps brachii

16- Brachioradialis
17- Extensor carpi radialis
    brevis
18- Extensor digitorum
    communis
19- Extensor carpi ulnaris
20- Flexor cruris medialis
21- Gastrocnemius brevis
22- Gastrocnemius external head
23- Flexor cruris lateralis
24- Lateralis caudae
25- Iliotibialis lateralis
26- Adductor pollicis longus
27- Flexor carpi ulnaris
28- Latissimus dorsi
29- Infraspinatus
30- Trapezius
31- Trapezius volatus

PLATE 7

1- *Quadratus lumborum*
2- *Gluteus medius*
3- *Rectus abdominis*
4- *Obliquus externus abdominis*
5- *Intercostalis externus*
6- *Intercostalis internus*
7- *Pectoralis major*
8- *Furculum ligament*
9- *Trapezius*
10- *Sternocleidomastoideus*

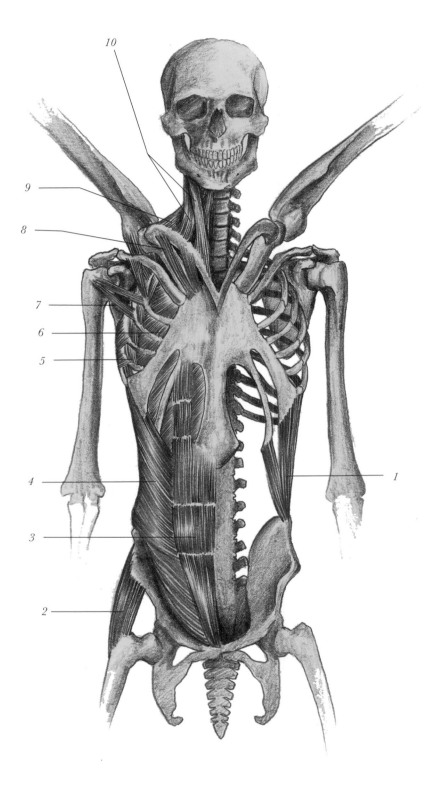

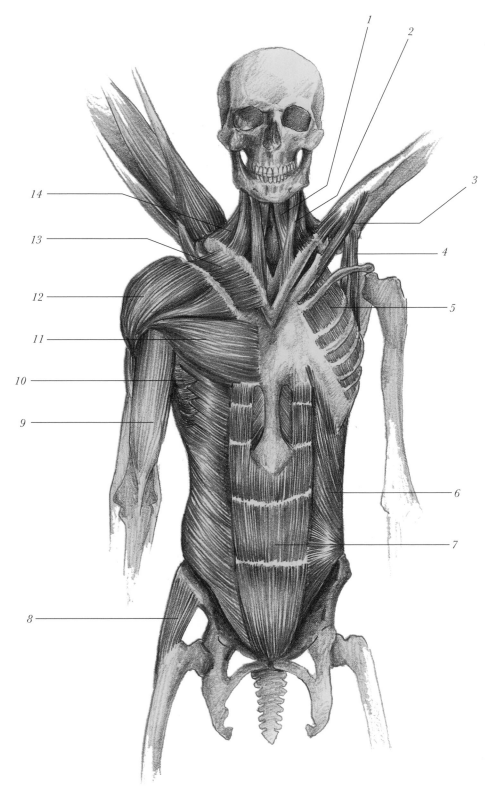

PLATE 8

1- *Sternohyoideus*
2- *Sternocleidomastoideus*
3- *Pectoralis thoracis brevis*
4- *Latissimus dorsi caudalis*
5- *Intercostalis internus*
6- *Obliquus externus abdominis*
7- *Rectus abdominis*
8- *Gluteus medius*
9- *Biceps brachii*
10- *Serratus*
11- *Pectoralis major*
12- *Deltoideus*
13- *Furculus intercostalis externus*
14- *Trapezius*

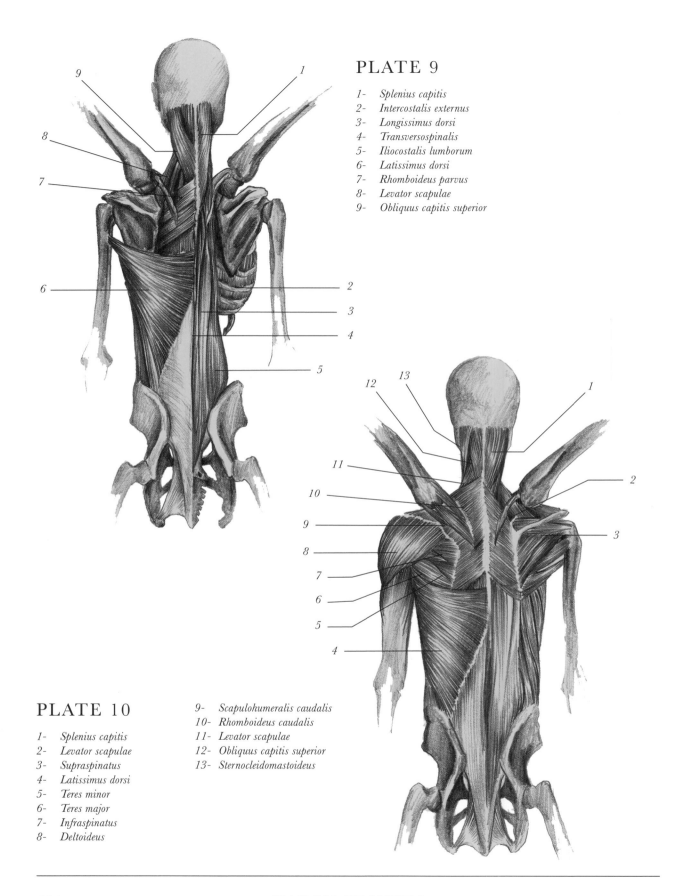

PLATE 9

1- *Splenius capitis*
2- *Intercostalis externus*
3- *Longissimus dorsi*
4- *Transversospinalis*
5- *Iliocostalis lumborum*
6- *Latissimus dorsi*
7- *Rhomboideus parvus*
8- *Levator scapulae*
9- *Obliquus capitis superior*

PLATE 10

1- *Splenius capitis*
2- *Levator scapulae*
3- *Supraspinatus*
4- *Latissimus dorsi*
5- *Teres minor*
6- *Teres major*
7- *Infraspinatus*
8- *Deltoideus*
9- *Scapulohumeralis caudalis*
10- *Rhomboideus caudalis*
11- *Levator scapulae*
12- *Obliquus capitis superior*
13- *Sternocleidomastoideus*

HARPY ERINYES

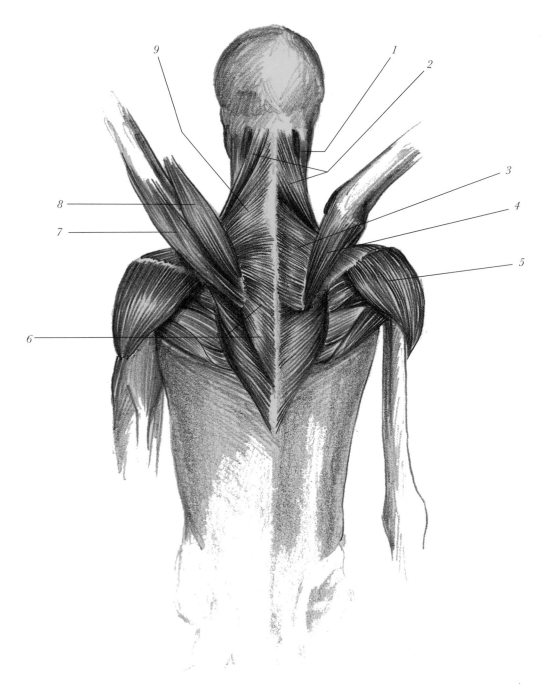

PLATE 11

1- *Sternocleidomastoideus*
2- *Trapezius*
3- *Rhomboideus caudalis*
4- *Deltoid minor*

5- *Deltoideus*
6- *Latissimus dorsi caudalis*
7- *Triceps brachii*
8- *Deltoid major*
9- *Trapezius caudalis*

HARPY ERINYES

185

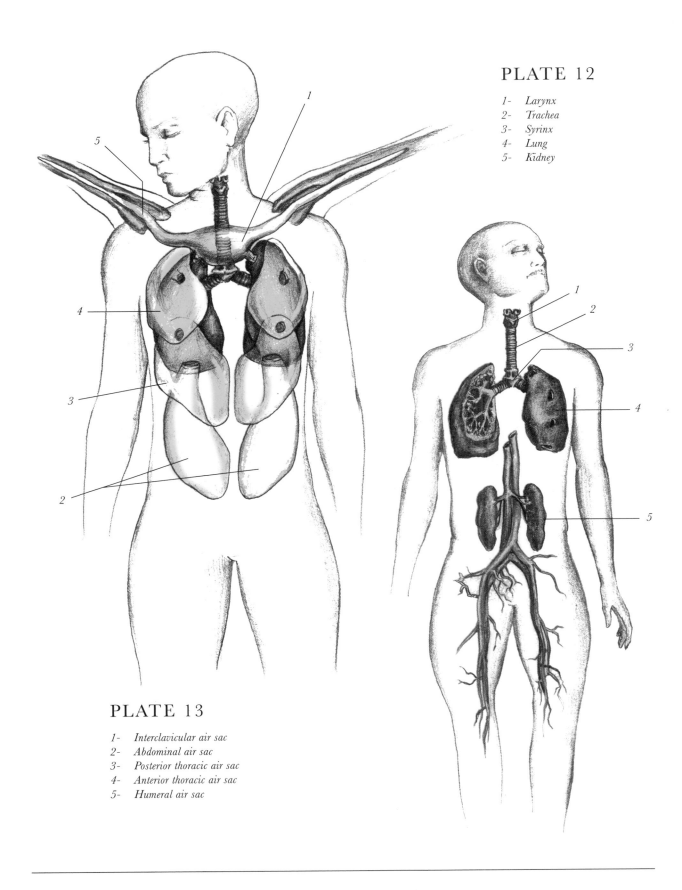

PLATE 12

1- *Larynx*
2- *Trachea*
3- *Syrinx*
4- *Lung*
5- *Kidney*

PLATE 13

1- *Interclavicular air sac*
2- *Abdominal air sac*
3- *Posterior thoracic air sac*
4- *Anterior thoracic air sac*
5- *Humeral air sac*

HARPY ERINYES

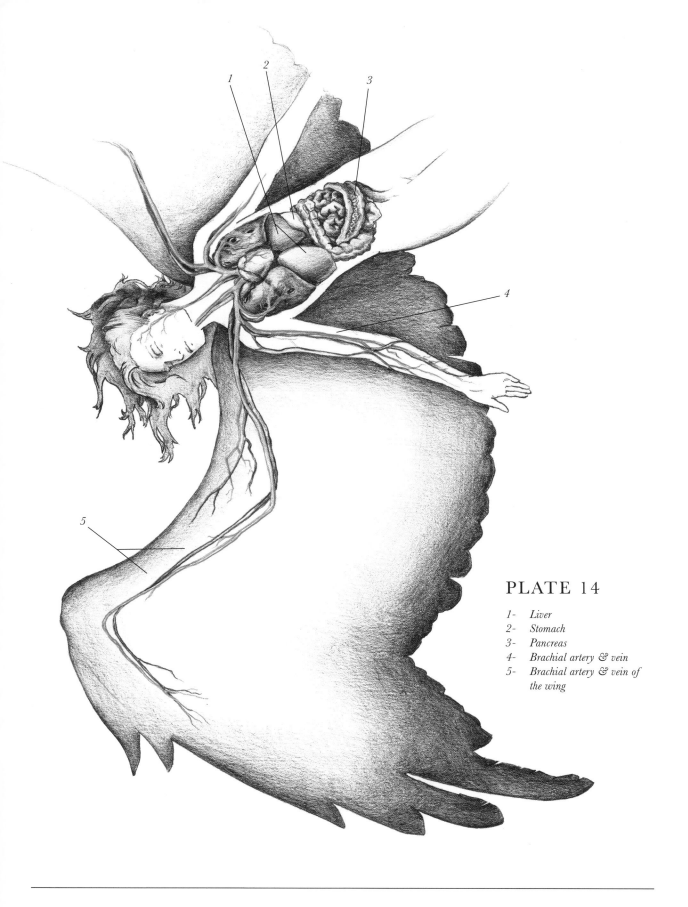

PLATE 14

1- *Liver*
2- *Stomach*
3- *Pancreas*
4- *Brachial artery & vein*
5- *Brachial artery & vein of the wing*

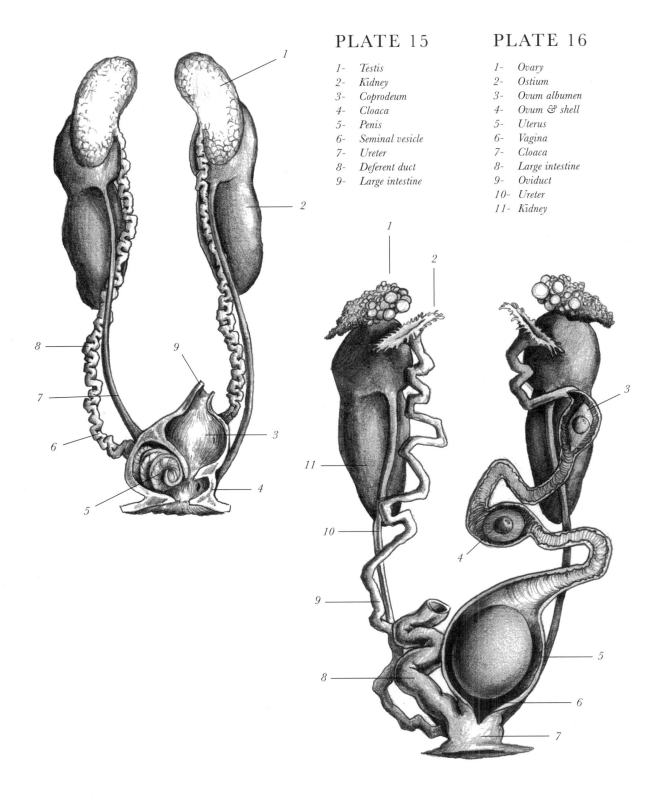

PLATE 15

1- *Testis*
2- *Kidney*
3- *Coprodeum*
4- *Cloaca*
5- *Penis*
6- *Seminal vesicle*
7- *Ureter*
8- *Deferent duct*
9- *Large intestine*

PLATE 16

1- *Ovary*
2- *Ostium*
3- *Ovum albumen*
4- *Ovum & shell*
5- *Uterus*
6- *Vagina*
7- *Cloaca*
8- *Large intestine*
9- *Oviduct*
10- *Ureter*
11- *Kidney*

PLATE 17

Embryo at 3 days

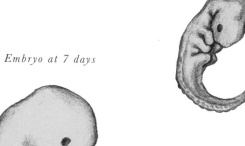

Embryo at 7 days

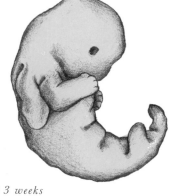

Harpy egg

Embryo at 3 weeks

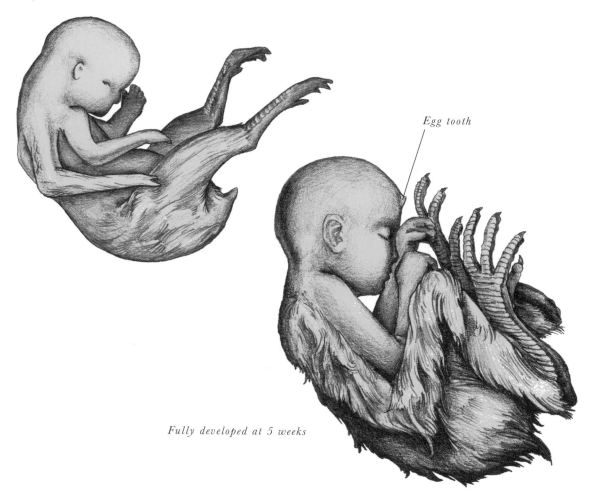

Egg tooth

Fully developed at 5 weeks

HARPY ERINYES

PLATE 18

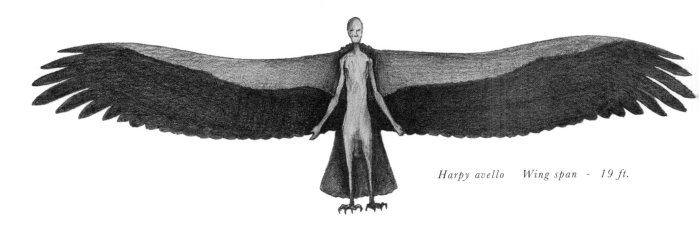

Harpy avello   Wing span - 19 ft.

Harpy erinyes   Wing span - 12 ft.

Harpy strophades   Wing span - 6 ft.

Harpy piorum   Wing span - 8 ft.

PLATE 19

A Final Note

Scholars seeking additional materials related to the life and work of Dr. Spencer Black will find a treasure trove of valuable resources at quirkbooks.com /theresurrectionist. This exclusive on-line content include a short film about this book, additional information about the creation of the illustrations, and digital imagery which may be downloaded for academic research and personal use. We encourage you to share your thoughts and ideas when visiting the site.